To Nick Royle

THE BOOK COLLECTOR

COLLECTOR

Alice Thompson

SALT

CROMER

PUBLISHED BY SALT
12 Norwich Road, Cromer, Norfolk NR27 0AX United Kingdom

© Alice Thompson, 2015

The right of Alice Thompson to be identified as the author of this
work has been asserted by her in accordance with Section 77 of the
Copyright, Designs and Patents Act 1988.

Printed in Great Britain by Clays Ltd, St Ives plc

Typeset in Sabon 10/13

ISBN 978 1 78463 043 0 paperback

1 3 5 7 9 8 6 4 2

THE BOOK COLLECTOR

Chapter 1

S HE WAITED, SITTING on the window seat, for the carriage to drive up the long avenue to their country house. Violet was looking forward to her husband Archie's return from London. The daffodils that bordered the driveway held their golden heads still. Later, a servant would perhaps bring them drinks in the drawing room, and Archie would lounge back in the velvet wing chair by the fire as he told her all about his day at work. As she waited she could hear, from the nursery, the baby crying again.

Archie had come into her life over a year ago. They had met by chance. She had been sitting at an outside table in a small artisan café off Oxford Circus, reading a book. She had been wearing one of her late mother's best hobble skirts that had accentuated her waist, and a delicate cerise blouse. A middle-aged man had sat down at an adjoining table, in a quick agile movement, as if on impulse. It was this apparent intuitiveness that had at first attracted her to him.

'What is the book you are reading?' he asked, before ordering a coffee from the waiter.

She had looked up at him but he had not smiled. He had just stared at her with relentless eyes, not looking at her, but straight through to her thoughts. At that moment, she felt she could never be anywhere else but here again.

'It's a book my parents gave me,' she replied, holding his gaze. She did not add that she had recently lost them both.

She tried to hold on to the details of his face but could only decipher a certain ponderousness that weighed down his symmetrical open features and clouded his dark blue eyes.

'You seem very young. How old are you?'

'Nineteen.'

'So what brings you to London?'

'I've just come in from Camberwell. I've come to look for work. Perhaps in one of the dress shops.'

'I wish you luck,' he said.

Was he flirting with her? She wasn't sure. His language sounded flirtatious but he appeared serious. She noticed his nails had been bitten down to the quick and the fingertips were tobacco stained.

He looked at her. 'Rose. Rose,' he repeated. 'By any other name.'

'It's not my name,' she replied.

Inexplicably, she knew she had to leave. Where had that brief, arbitrary exchange of words come from? As if their thoughts had been meeting in the air between them. She felt perturbed, not quite frightened. She carefully placed her half-drunken coffee cup down on the checked tablecloth, then turned round in her seat for her wide brimmed, battered felt hat that was balancing precariously on the back of her chair. Standing, she picked up her book from the table. Without catching his eye, she started to weave in and out of the outdoor tables back onto the pavement.

As she walked around the corner and out of sight, she felt surprised by a sense of loss. How could she be experiencing such a sensation of disappointment over a stranger? A small ivory card fell out of her book and fluttered onto the pavement. Violet picked it up to see it was a business card, printed in black ornate calligraphy, for a second-hand bookshop called Looking Glass. A Lord Archie Murray was the proprietor. He must have slipped the card inside the pages of her book when her back had been turned.

She pocketed the card and spent the rest of the day fruitlessly looking for work but it didn't occur to her to visit his bookshop. It was just another man showing interest in her; it meant nothing, after all.

On her way back to the railway station, she decided to take a short cut through an arcade. It wasn't a route that she normally took. There, halfway down the arcade, was a bookshop and she knew what its name would be before she could read the clear lettering on its frontage. But what made her decide to go in? She was intrigued by his interest in her. Should that have warned her off, rather than piqued her curiosity? But she was the sort of person who would invariably be drawn to a man's attentiveness. Fate and character conspiring together, playmates playing tag with each other, taking turns to play 'It'.

Circumstance. Impulse. Desire. They all drew her to the door and placed her leather-gloved hand on the dull brass door handle. Just another unconscious decision unconcerned with its irrevocable consequences, a choice that would determine the rest of her life.

CHAPTER 2

VIOLET OPENED THE door, which set off the clanging of a bell hanging from the ceiling. The room was dimly lit. The bookshop was divided by many rows of towering bookcases. Every shelf was laden with old books. Piles of ancient leather-bound books were also heaped up on the floor. A moss-green carpet, faded and worn, was just visible beneath the clutter. There was the overarching smell of dry must.

A young man was sitting on a stool in the corner at the far end of the bookshop, reading a book. He looked a few years older than her. His eyes were very dark and his skin had a pale lustre, like mother-of-pearl. His golden hair was curled close to his head like a cherub. He glanced up as she came in. Instead of saying 'Can I help you?' he simply returned to reading his book, as if he hadn't registered her. Unsure of her next step, she decided to browse the shelves. The books were arranged miscellaneously: Botanical, Anatomical and Ornithological all propped up next to each other.

She took out a book at random and opened it up at an anatomical drawing of a naked woman. Etched in fine ink-black lines, the body had been stripped of skin. The muscular tissue of the woman's breasts were like the elaborate swirling of cartographic mountains.

'They don't look like what they are, do they?'

She gave a start. The voice came from just over her shoulder. It was the low direct voice of the shop assistant. She turned to find him standing right behind her. There was a mischievous, indecent, wild look to him. She took a step back.

'They're just drawings,' she said, closing the book and putting the book back on the shelf.

'It's interesting,' he said, 'when people draw reality in lines – make it schematic without flesh or colour. It's like the skeleton of a fish. You can see the structure but it tells you nothing about how their scales flash silver in the sun. Or how they move and jump, poised in the air like apostrophes.'

'I wondered if Lord Murray was in?' she asked.

A petulant look crossed his face at her refusal to engage in his paradoxical conversation.

'He hasn't got back yet. He's been out most of the day. Would you like to leave a message for him?'

He had an odd scent about him. What was it? It was sweet and flowery like honey. He seemed too vivid, like all his desires were on display. But when he had been reading, he had seemed so intact, as if he had given himself over to the interior world of the book.

'Just tell him that Rose paid him a call.'

His expression changed immediately to one of severity. The mischievousness had left him.

'Is that supposed to be humorous? If so, I don't find it funny.'

Violet was bewildered. 'It's Lord Murray's humour. Rose is just the name he called me.'

'Well, I don't understand. I can see by your face you have no idea. Rose is the name of his late wife.'

Violet was speechless. A surge of protectiveness and empathy welled up inside her; Archie had suffered such pain and survived. It explained everything, she thought, why she had felt a vague unease in his presence. He was protecting his grief, as if it were a tender bloom that needed to flower fully before he could finally pick it and appreciate its perfume and the sensuous beauty of its silky white petals.

She wondered if the death of Archie's wife explained the sense she had received in the café that Archie was somehow separate from the rest of the world. Her heart went out to him. She would be patient. Already she was imagining how their love would grow, how they would have a different kind of bond together, indissoluble and strong.

The shop assistant was looking at her. 'Actually, now I look at you, I can see a slight resemblance, which might explain his actions. She had a kind of inconspicuous beauty that crept up on you when you weren't looking. It was more to do with who she was.' There was a look of such tender grief in his eyes as he said this, Violet suddenly wondered if he had been in love with Rose himself. The man's expression changed to one of detachment, as if the thought of Rose had obviated thoughts of anything else. He was looking at Violet as if she were an object.

'Have you got an address?' he asked.

He sounded practised. Did Archie have many women, since the death of his wife, visiting his bookshop, she wondered?

'No,' she said, quickly. 'I might visit again, another time.'

'Do you want to take that book?'

'Oh.' She looked at the book still in her hands.

'No thanks.' It was too expensive anyway. She didn't need a book on anatomy.

But when she got home to Camberwell, she thought of her beloved parents who were no longer with her, and she wished she did not feel so alone.

Returning to the bookshop the following day had felt like taking the same step all over again. She knew that returning had involved another self-defining act but after that she had lost all ability to choose.

A few days later, she and Archie visited an art gallery together. The paintings of contemporary significant figures in science, politics and the arts looked down at them. She caught her reflection in the glass of one of the portraits, her face superimposed onto the heavy bearded face of Edward Elgar. She could make out the oval shape of her face, her large dark eyes, the narrow stubborn chin. She looked round to see Archie smiling at her, as if knowing what she was doing.

'You can see your face in the glass,' she had said.

'Indeed you can,' he said. She could see in his eyes that he liked what he saw.

Their romance had been like a fairy tale. She felt that if only she could work out which fairy tale it was, it would somehow help her. They rarely spoke – just to be in each other's presence was enough. Previously, when she had visited cafes on her own, she had become overwhelmed by people's chatter. But now she was with Archie, what they shared together didn't need words. Their attraction operated in silence. Why would you need words when you could read each other's thoughts and desires?

All that existed was his desire for her. She felt consumed and overwhelmed. This feeling was new, frightening and unnatural. All she could think about was him. He attended to her every need, and anticipated her wishes as if he could read her mind. It was enchanting.

A month after their first meeting he asked her to marry him; it had seemed inevitable. She had allowed him to enter her life, embraced him, without question. And he had somehow understood her receptiveness, picked up on it by silent instinct. His need of her and her response had been a perfect match.

However, she sensed an inherent danger in this equivalence, in the hidden closeness of their intimacy and understanding. That what lay underneath was real, but the equally attractive surface was an illusion like a mirage of water on desert sand. She had been beguiled by appearance, by Archie's charm and attractiveness, how they looked together, his love for her. She had been like a child entering a world full of wonder and awe and excitement. It was an image that presented itself to her, of beauty and security. She had not asked herself why this imagery should have such power over her.

He too had lost his parents and had inherited, a couple of years ago, a small country estate just a few miles outside London. He never spoke of his dead wife and she never asked him about her.

Violet and Archie were married, without guests, at a registry office. Archie's gardener and an old school friend of his that Violet never saw again acted as witnesses. The morning after their wedding night, she woke up in his ancestral home, to see him lying next to her in their marriage bed, rumpled, unshaven and full of need. She bent over him and kissed him full on the mouth, bringing her hand down over his body, back and forth, high and low. He groaned and turned over and without opening his eyes reached for her.

She had never known such yearning and it was as if he had woken her up from slumber like Sleeping Beauty. His elusive nature offered up promises to her that could never be fulfilled, except for that brief orgasmic moment when everything finally did make sense. He had a voice that lulled her, sustained her, with its musical indifference to anything but his own wishes and desires.

CHAPTER 3

HAVING WAITED TOO long on the window seat for Archie's carriage to arrive, Violet went into the kitchen. She knew as lady of the house it was not where she belonged, but, when the cook and other servants were elsewhere, it was to where she always gravitated. It was a big room with a large table in the centre and a wooden dresser standing behind. Copper saucepans hung on the white-painted walls. She looked around at all the physical things and suddenly felt scared. Scared at the contrast between her emotions and all these things. Her emotions seemed incoherent but the physical reality of the world around her felt compact and self-contained.

She picked up a plate from the dresser and deliberately let it fall from her fingers onto the tiled floor. She heard the sound of the crack, saw it break into three pieces. It was one of the ancestral plates, precious, with the crest of a lion. Was it a coincidence that she had broken one of his precious ancestral plates or was it *because* it was one of the precious ancestral plates that she had deliberately let it slip from her fingers?

She bent down and picked up the pieces and wrapped them in newspaper and carefully placed them in the sink. She wondered if Archie would notice if a plate had gone missing. Or if he would be cross if she told him the truth. Material possessions meant a great deal to him. She had learnt during the short time they had been married how much physical things mattered to him. As if things symbolised the emotions he couldn't have. And this plate would symbolise the most practical and simplest of losses. But she loved him, always struggled with her love for him. For if there was one defining quality about her, it was her loyalty.

Later that evening, she took a luxurious bath. As she listened to some music on the gramophone she told herself how lucky she was to have her husband, her baby and this wonderful house, before retiring to bed. She heard Archie get in late, heard his steps on the stairs, felt the weight of his body shift down on the mattress as he got into bed, but she didn't respond as he cuddled up to her back. She pretended to be asleep, and a few moments later she could hear his deep unconscious breathing.

Many years later, looking back, she was amazed at the capacity we have for not wanting to confront the truth. How the humdrum of our own lives, the security of habit and comfort, prevent us from questioning the clues and hints that the truth gives us. We can ignore them, make excuses and forget whatever we want.

She extricated herself from the sheets and went into the nursery. She listened to the baby's soft breathing as he slept, the sweet rhythms. She softly stroked his naked back so as not to wake him. Looking at him she felt her nipples prick with leaking milk. These constantly soporific, sensuous days of Felix sleeping, waking, crying, breastfeeding, she had never felt more of an insensate animal. Archie was like a cut-out shadow moving in and out of rooms while her new identity, of giving flesh, warm milk, soothing soft hands, was her undulating reality.

Felix woke up and seeing her face started to cry. He can read my mind, she thought, he can read my mind. She realised the truth, that she was not the one with the power – it was Felix.

As a bookshop owner, Archie was a bibliophile. He collected books, generally valuable first editions, for his own private collection, too. Their house was becoming more and more full of books. He would buy books and bring them back, like a hunter bringing back the corpses of small animals. They were books that Archie never read. He liked them as objects that he could arrange in alphabetical order or by subject. Her favourites were esoteric books on alchemy, astronomy and anatomy. She would examine the line drawing of a man heating lead in a crucible over a crozier and take pleasure in its diagrammatic portrayal of madness, obsession, and intellectual curiosity.

One evening, Violet watched Archie in his library as he picked up a book and stroked his finger lingeringly over its leather cover. She watched as he opened it and brought up the splayed yellowing pages to his nostrils. He slowly inhaled. It was sensual, her husband's experience of books, the texture, the sweet or acrid odours, the feel of a rough, uncut page.

She thought they had shared the same love of books; it was one of the reasons she had fallen in love with him. But it was the content she loved, the processes of thought, the flight of imagination. She was not interested in the texture of old leather or the condensed pulp of fallen trees.

Somewhere, instinctually, she felt the two were exclusive, that Archie's fetishistic appraisal of a book betokened his lack of interest in thought. She knew this was not necessarily true but the odd way he lingered over the book without reading any of the words made her wonder what else this obsession precluded. If his obsession precluded meaning, did it also preclude herself and their new baby?

'You are treating that book like a lover,' she teased.

'Once I have owned a book I am longing for the next one. Collecting is a creative act. One of perpetual longing and desire. One is never fully fulfilled. Collectors live in dread of satisfaction. There is that brief, transitory moment of satisfaction and then it disappears like dust in the air. We live to long after something, we know and accept the power of longing and desire. We are under no illusion that what we want is the unobtainable.'

'You still sound in love.'

'What you mean, don't you, is that I am misguided and deluded, like a lover? As if another object or creature could ever fulfil all your dreams! Even for a moment.'

Flicking through the catalogue of books in the library a week later in its thick heavy red binder with gold lettering, she wondered what book she would choose to read next. A book entitled Fairy Tales by Hans Christian Andersen had been listed in Archie's clear slanted handwriting and then marked by a single black seal. Curious, she tried to find the book in the library. She looked under fiction, then myths, as it clearly was a special book, but could find it nowhere. When Archie returned from work that evening, she asked him where the book was.

'I keep it in my safe.'

'Can I see it?' She could tell he didn't want to talk about it. 'Why won't you let me see it?' she asked, but he shrugged his shoulders.

'The book won't interest you. And it needs to be kept out of the light. Sunlight damages the pages. Makes the print fade.'

'It does interest me. I like fairy stories. You know I do.'

Violet had loved fairy tales as a little girl, their dark iciness striking her as containing truths about life. There was a purity of emotion about them whether it was of love, hate or desire.

Even when she was a child, they made her feel they were more real to her than the daily poverty of her life, her father a cobbler, struggling to bring home to their rented rooms enough money for his family to live on.

'I've told you. I don't want the book damaged.' He was treating her like a child.

And then he fobbed her off with a promise, offering up the future to her instead.

'In a few weeks I'll show it to you. It needs special gloves.'

But she never saw the book. It was kept in the safe, the safe that was somewhere in his study, but she did not know where.

As Archie ran his hands over her body that night she remained distant and objective. She could hear the baby was crying again. She felt vulnerable, her skin irritable. Desire had changed to various other emotions, like a chameleon, she thought, evasive and slippery. She wanted it all over with and, as he came, an odd feeling of distance overwhelmed her, as if he had become a stranger. So he had secrets? Well, she could have secrets, too.

Chapter 4

S HE LOOKED OUT of the window. The flowers were just coming into bloom. The lush white blooms of the *prunus*, the hallucinating acid green of the budding leaves. The birds in their cacophony for a mate. They just were.

She couldn't get the fairy tale book out of her mind. She looked around at her exquisite house and the garden. How far away from her past she now seemed. This was what was real now. The substance of materialised wealth, it protected her from everything, including herself. She managed the household, supervised the staff and looked after Felix. She loved her husband and her family was everything to her. Her way of life here was her whole identity – to question the reality of her life was to question the reality of her being. She had little realisation at the time of what she was doing, no idea that she was turning her back on anything.

In the past month, since Violet had found out about the book in the safe, Archie had become diffuse round the edges like the prints on the walls. He had started to come back even later at night. He looked the same as usual, slim, chestnut haired, apparently friendly and open, yet also intractable. He was equitable. But he had lost his specificity. He appeared enthusiastic but something in him had gone missing. Archie had become uncircumscribed. It was as if Violet had offered him a definition by marrying him that he was now resisting.

But only on the inside. On the outside he was just the same. Was that what Archie was now doing in their lives? Pretending to be who he was?

The world started to seem dangerous to her and Felix. She began to see danger all around. Everything seemed poised to take Felix away from her. It was as if the universe, just as it had created him, was now designed to take him away from her. She became convinced just as she had been gifted Felix, so, too, she would be punished by his loss.

She decided to find out more about the book of fairy tales. One day when Archie was planning to be back from London late, this provided the impetus she needed. He would be late, so she would disobey him. Childish, this tit-for-tat? No. It was about finding out the truth.

She went into his dark green study, the windows obscured by the heavy golden curtains. It would be behind his favourite picture in the study. She looked behind the oil painting of the nude Venus but there was nothing but a darker square of green where the painting had protected the wall from the light. Then perhaps the safe was behind the landscape painting of the grounds and house? She lifted the painting completely off the wall and leant it carefully against the desk. Behind, inserted in the wall, was the metal door of his safe. But how to find out the combination of the safe? It would be a series of numbers. She tried Archie's date of birth. She tried Felix's. She finally tried hers. The safe opened. She was surprised he had used that date. Lying inside was the book.

The book had a pale green binding of calfskin. The outline of a white circle had been inserted in the front. The book looked old. She opened it up. The illustrations were printed in bright colours. The girls' faces had a flat look with the luminous big eyes and curly golden hair of Victorian times. What was so special about it? Why had he locked *this* book in the safe? It was a first edition but Archie had many first editions in his library. The pages were thick with gilt edges. She looked at the flyleaf: *For Rose*. It was dated just before they had met.

Violet let out a gasp of shock and bewilderment. So this was why he had kept it secret from her. This book was a token of love for his dead wife.

She heard the front door open and she quickly put the book back in the safe and shut the door. She could hear his footsteps in the corridor as she hung the picture back on the wall. She turned round to see Archie come into the study, his usual exuberant self. Her heart went out to him in spite of herself. How she looked forward to him coming back home after work. How, in the hours before, anticipation of his coming would swell up unconsciously and creep into her mind like a cat slowly approaching a bird. He moved like a cat, she thought, sinuous and effective, and that made her the bird, a little blackbird with beady eyes.

'How was your day?' she asked. 'You are back earlier than you said you would be.'

'I was tired, so I changed my plans.'

Was it her imagination or did his eye flick over to the painting? She made an effort not to follow his eyes. Had she hung the painting back on the wall straight?

'How was work?'

'Fine. Are you all right? You look tired.'

'There's no need to treat me like an invalid.'

'Sorry.'

She fought against his concern that since the birth of their baby she hadn't felt quite herself. Beneath this apparent idyll where everything on the surface seemed so perfect, where the birds sang and the trees were inexorably growing into bud, there was a certain fear, all along. Fear was growing as surely as the buds were unfolding. A secret, hidden budding fear, curled up in on itself, waiting for the sun to shine on it, for it to unfold. But until that happened she wouldn't let the light shine on it, just as the book stayed locked up in the safe, hidden away.

CHAPTER 5

A S SHE WATCHED the leaves on the trees turn greener, this odd paralysing fear remained resolutely folded up on itself. This desire not to know the truth. It was an odd kind of self-preservation.

But looking back, she was right to protect herself from the truth. The truth was to do her damage. And look how the sunlight illuminated the garden. The sun now after a particularly cold winter. But in an odd way the heat, the unfamiliar heat after the cold, added a kind of nervous strain to her, for it signalled change.

Friends did visit, however. One in particular was Bea, a grey-haired spinster who lived in the neighbouring village, just a mile from the estate. She bounced in one day, full of energy in spite of being well over seventy and with a disarming child-like self-absorption that came from having only herself to look after. She plonked herself down at the kitchen table.

Her first words to Violet were, 'You look different.'

'I do? In what way?'

'More there, somehow.'

'Unlike being somewhere else.'

Why were personal comments about her making her feel so defensive? Bea was kindness itself – she bore no malice.

'You look as if something is intriguing you.'

Violet couldn't help but laugh.

'Am I that obvious? I can't seem to stop thinking about it.'

'Thinking about what?'

'Oh, this book. Archie has hidden a book of fairy tales away in his safe. And won't let me see it.'

'So how do you know about it?'

'I opened his safe.'

Bea looked aghast and impressed at the same time.

'You are a dark horse, Violet.'

'But I've decided it's nothing.'

'You've decided it's nothing. What happens if it's not nothing? What happens if it's something?'

Violet was beginning to feel unaccountably angry. She looked across at Bea and could see the whirring of her thoughts.

She looked out of the window. It was another beautiful early March day. Everything was clear and fresh. She didn't want anything to change.

'It is nothing, Bea. I don't know why I told you anything about it. It's just his possessiveness and secretiveness. I wasn't going to tell you this but he has dedicated the book to Rose!'

Bea gave her an odd look.

'Did you ever meet Rose?' Violet asked.

'I did, briefly. She died soon after they moved here. She was absolutely lovely. In all ways. In the most important ways.'

'How did she die?'

'It was tragic. In childbirth. The baby died with her.'

'And how did Archie take it?'

'It struck him very hard. But he's never one to give himself away. Do you not find Archie's desire to collect odd?'

'What do you mean?'

'Obsessive.'

'It's what he likes to do.'

'You don't think it means he's missing something?'

'I don't understand.'

Bea laughed and crossed her sturdy legs, thick as oak trunks in their jodhpurs. She nursed her cup in her large familiar hands.

'I can't explain exactly. It just seems a bit cold.'

'No, I know what you mean. But he's not like that really. He's kind.'

'Are you sure? The birth has taken a lot out of you. It's only been a month and you imagine that people have qualities they don't have. The ones you have too much of.'

'I'm not kind.'

'You're sensitive. That's your trouble. And susceptible. You trust people too much.'

'Are you saying I shouldn't trust Archie?'

'No, not exactly. I don't know what I mean. I shouldn't have brought it up. I'm being silly.'

'No, you shouldn't. You've never liked Archie. I think you secretly find him attractive.'

Bea laughed, her grey curls trembling. 'Like anything.'

In spite of her anger, Violet felt relieved, in a way, that she had told Bea about the book. It was out in the open.

'It's not just going to disappear, you know that,' Bea said.

'What?'

'Your knowledge about the book. You have it now. Whatever you do with it.'

Just at that moment they heard the front door open. It was Archie.

They listened to his footsteps as he walked down the corridor towards them. The kitchen door opened. There he was at the entrance, looking handsome and open faced with his natural engaging smile. The few grey flecks in his brown, wavy hair gave him gravity. None of this is making any sense, Violet thought. Nothing adds up. I can't get things to cohere.

She felt feelings of love and pride and undying loyalty to Archie as he stood there. He was true; he belonged to her.

'Good afternoon, Bea,' he said. Still that smile – you couldn't tell that he didn't like her. But they circled around each other like predator and prey. Violet could almost see the hairs rise on Bea's arms when he walked into the room. They were obviously civil to each other but Archie had a male pride that found Bea's dominant nature unfeminine. Violet knew her own introversion had appealed to him, since it made no demands on him, but Bea on the other hand – Violet could see Archie found the strident urgency of her mind oppressive.

They sat round the table talking about the unexpectedly warm weather for the time of year until Bea finally left. Violet went out onto the lawn and lay down in the prickly grass amongst the daisies. It had been a long winter and now this sun. It beat down on her face and on her limbs. Everything was going to be all right, she thought. How can it not be on this fine afternoon, with the pigeons cooing and sensation gradually returning to all her limbs?

But then her body went rigid. Transparent and veiled, the garden seemed to take on a grey mist and a languor came over her. Something in her life, her precious, idyllic existence, was wrong. This sensation was trying to tell her something. It was a warning, like a prophecy. It was all to do with the book in the safe. And she felt as she lay there that her limbs and her eyelids were heavy and her skin on fire.

Just then she heard Felix gurgle in his pram on the lawn. And it felt as if someone were pulling her out of the grey, back into the garden with the lawns and beds full of flowers. The cooing pigeons gradually became more audible again. She went over to the pram and looked down at Felix. He lifted up his round chubby arms towards her and the fog drifted away and only the vague traces of doom outlined her heart.

She saw his open, pale face, the eyes the colour of two small coals and the thin intelligent lips. The freckles that dusted his nose, freckles that she once had thought had been added, to give the illusion that he was a real child when really he was a changeling.

Chapter 6

That evening, in the library, she took down from a shelf a book on anatomy. She started to skim through it. The picture of a body being flayed caught her eye. Hanging upside down, by chains, by his feet. It was a cadaver in an anatomy class. A convict perhaps, hanged upside down on a star-shaped board. His legs and arms outstretched like a four-pronged star. A man was intent on flaying his arm with a knife. Violet realised with a shock that the sketcher had drawn the man alive. She briefly tried to imagine how it would be, to be flayed like Marsyas.

She heard the door open and Archie come in. She turned round to greet him. He had an expression on his face she had never seen before. It was a distorted look that made his flesh seem mobile, as if the skin were melting. She immediately realised he had found out that she had opened his safe, that she had discovered the fairy tale book. He rushed over and snatched the anatomy book from her hands. He began nervously fingering its pages.

'Don't ever go into the safe again without consulting me. I could see the fairy tale book had been put back in a different position.'

'I'm sorry.'

'Don't you realise how precious that book is?'

'But books are meant to be read!'

'Not that one.'

'Because it's for Rose?'

He looked as if he were about to slap her. 'How do you know that? Don't you dare mention her name to me. You don't understand. Books have to be cared for, looked after. Otherwise they will be damaged. In fact, I forbid you to go into the library as well!'

This onslaught, she felt, was damaging their marriage, its irrationality far more significant than what it was about.

'But what am I to do – I love reading – if I am at the house all day?'

'You can embroider, play music. Besides, you have the baby to care for. And you refuse all help. Why you won't have a nanny is beyond me. It's most irregular. I don't understand it.'

'I want to look after him myself.'

'Don't worry. Felix will be safe. I've told you before. I know someone who has been recommended. A Clara Whittaker.'

'No,' she said. 'No. Things happen with nannies. Children drown in streams. It's not the same as them having their mother.'

'You mean nannies don't fuss.'

'Yes, that is what I do mean. Why do you think mothers fuss? It's evolutionary. It protects their young.'

'Clara would be a boon. I hear she's very good. Responsible. She has two younger brothers that she helped to bring up.'

'Why would I want a stranger looking after my baby? She might harm him.'

'Look after Felix then, if it's what you want to do! But please don't touch any of my books again.'

'Can I not even read the ones in the library? I promise I won't look in the safe again.'

'No. Not even them. You might stain them with the sweat on your hands.'

He was making her feel as if his books were more precious to him than she was. She suddenly felt like an imposter, the way Archie had plucked her from obscurity to marry her. Really, she was an interloper in this house full of beautiful *objets d'art* and discreet servants.

He saw the anguish on her face. He quickly regained his composure. She could see he realised he had stepped over the mark, gone beyond whatever Archie considered was acceptable behaviour in their marriage.

'I'm sorry, dearest. I didn't mean to upset you. You must realise how important my books are. They are irreplaceable.' She felt relieved, even grateful for his remorse.

'Of course I understand. I shouldn't have gone into your safe and I won't go into the library again.'

She left the library astonished, wondering how an argument could have been conjured out of something that seemed to be far more to do with Archie than with her. For weeks now her domestic life had lacked fluency and she realised it was because on some level she had become unhappy. And unhappiness had made her life like a river, consistently coming up against rocks that had to be circumvented or obstacles that impeded its flow.

That evening at dinner, she looked at her husband through the candlelight. She tried to reframe him as someone different and could not. He was her husband. She cherished him. He protected and loved her; how she adored his body. The way his chestnut hair swept back from his forehead, his handsome older face. She was devoted and could not imagine disloyalty in others. Looking back, it had been a failure of her imagination or perhaps a failure of her nature. Or perhaps of both. It was too hard to try and see him in a new way and she would not.

In her bedroom, the moon was shining through the window

full and strong. Whereas a few months before she would have cried at her argument with Archie, now she just felt a little hardening of the heart and a painful constriction, as if she were becoming less generous and kind, turning into a smaller person. She felt his secrecy about the book, his compulsion to keep all his books to himself, was driven by desire, a sexual possessiveness. She remembered the way sometimes he caressed his books.

After Archie left for work the next day, she entered the library and continued to peruse the books. Drifting from one book to another, looking at the etchings of Dürer or reading the philosophy of Rousseau, or the fiction of George Eliot, she read for the prose style or for information or for both until her eyes grew tired. But she was now careful of the books and nervously tender with them, until, lost in the prose, she forgot what she was handling and began to turn the pages roughly. She was always careful to put the books back exactly where she found them, which was straightforward as they were so carefully ordered alphabetically and arranged in categories.

CHAPTER 7

ONE NIGHT SHE woke up with her back towards Archie. She turned round to see, instead of him, an empty space and rumpled sheets. The blankets had been cast back and there was an indentation in the mattress where his body should have been. She had the overwhelming feeling he had secretly left the house. And to her shock, looking over at the chair where he normally folded his clothes, she saw that they had gone. The next morning, she didn't say anything, as if somehow she knew that if she asked questions, confronted him, he would disappear in front of her.

The next night, she tried to stay awake, to see if she could catch him leaving. But she drifted off and then woke up, startled, in the middle of the night. She quickly turned over. Archie was sleeping beside her. She turned back over and dug her nails into her palm to keep herself awake. Ten minutes later she heard him quietly get out of the bed and dress, tiptoeing cautiously about the room, so as not to wake her. She heard him softly close the door. Moments later, she leapt out of bed, flung on her dress and shoes, and followed him outside into the cool night. She caught sight of him walking down the driveway, a lonely and estranged figure. For a mile she followed him through the darkness.

He began to walk faster, possessed, as if the devil had

appeared at his heels. He was walking along the road in the direction of the asylum, a nineteenth-century dilapidated institution that had been built on the far side of the village surrounded by its own private estate. Just as he was at the edge of the asylum's estate, he suddenly vanished. Violet halted on the road, tried to remain calm, but he had dissipated entirely into the thin night air. There was just the black landscape of the countryside all around and a full moon in the sky, obscured momentarily by clouds. Wondering if it had all been a mad dream, she returned home, clambered into bed and fell into a deep, dreamless sleep. When she awoke, Archie was lying beside her, as if he had always been there.

Seeing him sleeping there, she felt riven by desire. The possibility of losing him suddenly seemed to become a certainty. She bent over and kissed him, made love to him, as if her heart would break. All the time she was aware of an unspokenness stopping up her mouth. She tried to fill up her mouth instead with his tongue, his lips. Anything rather than ask the words that would break the spell, uncover the truth she didn't want to know. Not now, when everything was skating on the surface of her survival.

Why did Archie have so much power over her? Was it a spell he had cast over her or a spell that she had cast over him? A spell that said, I give you power over me. She continued to resist asking him where he went to at night. His absences had become a regular occurrence. She didn't want the answer. She could sense that he was not just going for a walk because he couldn't sleep, that there was a purpose, an assignment that took him along the dark, straight lanes of the countryside, towards his destination. She could follow him, physically. But she would not ask him face to face or give him the opportunity to confound her with his lies, his eyes looking into hers, his power to deceive her at its most sensible and irrefutable.

No, better to match secrecy with secrecy, enter his realm of deception, that landscape of shadows and creation where following her errant husband into the night suddenly seemed not wrong or mad at all. In fact she had never felt more sane, as if what she was doing was the natural summation, conclusion, of this married life together, that the revelation of the hidden had been the end point of their marriage.

All that was obscure about him, then and now, had to be accepted. And she had to enter that obscurity, manipulate it to her own ends, bring it into the light. This was the only way to find out the truth. She would never be able to find out the truth on her terms – only on his. She would be outwitted unless she entered his world. What she chose to do, to secretly follow him, was no compromise. Quite the opposite, it was from a stance of strength, not a position of weakness, that she could do this. Afterwards she would be able to come out into the light, unscathed and untainted, like invisible ink appearing on an apparently blank page.

CHAPTER 8

A FEW NIGHTS later, she was trying to fall asleep, when she heard Archie quietly rise from the bed. She did not know what violence waited for her, what it would do to her, what she would do to it. Her plans to match his secrecy with her own fell away. She was unable any longer to contain her curiosity.

'Archie, where do you go to at night?'

He sat back down on the edge of the bed. Even in the darkness she could sense his calmness but she could also hear his hands were tapping on the frame of the bed: *tap tappety tap, tap tappety tap.*

'I don't go anywhere, darling.'

She turned on the gaslight by their bed. His eyes were resilient and watchful like a reptile.

'But I've seen you, Archie. You go out at night.' She didn't say that she had followed him to the edge of the asylum's estate, seen him vanish many times.

He suddenly looked wildly angry as if he had summoned up his anger out of nowhere.

'Have you been spying on me?'

'No, Archie. It's not like that at all. It's just I heard you get up.' She couldn't help but be defensive; it was in her nature.

'You know. I've told you when I can't sleep I go for a walk. It's what I always do.'

But he had just said that he didn't go anywhere. Or had he? She was growing confused. Archie, in the dim light of the room, straightened his back, pulled himself together; he was trying to look like an ordinary husband, she thought with a cold sense of shock.

'Come here, my darling.' He put his arms around her. She could smell his sweet scent. The scent that meant security, marital happiness, and her future mapped out in straight, unwavering lines of contentment. She inhaled deeply, his aroma relaxing her, making her feel calm. She could sense his body holding itself deliberately still, letting her inhale him, giving her the opportunity to feel safe in his arms. There was no fury here, no walls of shame.

It was only sex which brought her back to the physicality of herself. Was that why she needed it so much now? When she was ostracised from sex, she began to feel withered. She felt her body hunch up and she lost her appetite, as if she were fading away.

Amy liked to swim in the sea. She would take off her clothes. She swam deep down amongst the sand and shells, the starfish on the bottom, feeling like a mermaid. It was lovely to be so free after her confinement, the cold salty water engulfing her. She became confirmed. The cold water was refreshing and cleansing. She surfaced. She swam to the shore and strode up onto the sand. The warm air was gentle on her skin. Her skin was goose-pimpled with the cold, but the warm air gradually restored it to its original smoothness.

She didn't notice the person standing in the shadows watching her, in the shadow of the trees, admiring her white voluptuous body, its curves and undulations so conspicuous against the backdrop of the blue sea.

Her long blond hair was dripping over her shoulders and

down over her breasts. The watcher gasped at her sensual nonchalance. She turned to look at the sea. He could clearly see the curve of her buttocks, the deep cleft, her wide hips and narrow waist. She should dive back into the sea, he thought, that is where she belongs. Deep down in the water. He imagined her breathing under the water, like a mermaid living in a palace made of coral.

He came swiftly up behind her as she looked out at the sun setting over the sea, turning the water to gold. He locked an arm around her neck and then swiftly snapped his elbow to the right. He flung her over his shoulder and carried her through the forest into the tunnel carved in the rock face.

Inside the cave he began to prepare her body. It was one of the things that was important to the ritual. He lay her on the rocky ground. How beautiful she looked naked, her hair drying to its golden state. It was like spun gold, like a mermaid's hair. He washed her body carefully, so there was no salt on it, spoiling her skin. She was already quite clean because of the sea. He just had to remove the salt. Between the shoulder blades. Every indentation.

She was a beautiful object to him; how he admired it. She was soft flesh and hard bone and it gave him a thrill to move from one texture to another, at his will and at his own pace, but always with his final goal in mind, his single focus driving him, giving meaning to everything he was doing. He felt his heart beat faster with rising excitement as he was reaching the final stages of what he had to do. He turned her over and took out a knife. Making the incision of a rough circle, he peeled some skin from her back. How tender and soft it was. He then began to hack at her thighs, until the blood poured out from her.

Violet and Archie walked down the path to the beach lined by bluebells and primroses. She wanted to see the beach and the rocks that formed a naturally enclosed harbour. She needed to clear her mind. But halfway down the path she suddenly became overwhelmed by the conviction that something terrible had befallen Felix.

She ran back up the path, breathless, trampling over the flowers, through the garden, into the house. Felix was still lying peacefully asleep in his pram in the hallway. What was she finding sinister in the most innocuous, beautiful afternoon? What fairy tale had a missing child at the heart of it? She remembered the book of fairy tales in the study.

She felt her neck. There were marks where Archie had bitten her during their love making. She glanced at herself in the hallway mirror, with her long straggly hair, unkempt and hunched with anxiety, and didn't believe it was her.

Now she wondered what Archie had seen in her. Was it her susceptibility? But why? Where was the location of the deceit? She couldn't work it out. His masculine certainty against her vague feminine amorphousness would heal the uncertainty of her world. Make everything clear cut and understandable. Archies's perception of her was stronger and more certain and took precedence over her own view of herself as mother and wife. Like the tree falling in the forest, she was only falling because God was watching.

CHAPTER 9

IN THE EARLY evening light, Violet was in the drawing room enjoying watching Felix lying naked on the rug, his delicate fingers grasping the empty air. Suddenly, underneath his bare chest, she noticed a small fluid movement as if an insect was crawling under the surface. Unsure of what she had seen she kneeled down beside him. She gently turned him over and stifled a scream. Under the length of his back insects were scuttling under his skin, his flesh protruding in the shape of their tiny linear forms. He seemed innocently oblivious to what was happening. Hopelessly, she tried to brush them off but the insects were trapped under his skin. She could feel the shells of their bodies hard underneath her fingers. Felix was now crying in distress. The insects were hurting him. She would have to excise them, cut them out.

She began to frantically rub her hands over his skin trying to kill them. Felix was now screaming. Utter panic was choking her. *'It's all right, darling, hush, hush, I will get rid of them.'* Oh my God, he was so distressed.

Just then she heard Archie's footsteps come into the drawing room behind her.

'What the hell is going on?' he shouted at her over Felix's screams. He rushed over and grabbed Felix off the floor. Felix gradually calmed down in his arms.

Archie turned to her, furious. 'What have you done to him?'

'What do you mean?'

'Look at his back.'

He turned the baby around in his arms. His pink buttocks and back were covered in scratches that her fingernails had made.

'There were insects crawling under his skin. I had to get them out.' She was desperate to make him understand.

'Violet, you clearly are strained and exhausted. There are no insects under his skin. Go to bed and rest.' His angry look had been replaced by one of concern.

'No, I'm fine.' Bewildered, she could see, apart from the scratches, how smooth the baby's back was. Relief flooded her that the insects had gone. She put her arms out to take him. Felix looked at her with his knowing eyes and reached up his hand to her. She took it and kissed his baby fingers. The nails so tiny, like baby shells.

'You know I would never harm you,' she said. 'I am your mother.'

'He's probably hungry. And you fussing over him probably just distressed him more.' But Archie didn't hand the baby over to her.

She went up and leant her head on his strong shoulder.

'Really, Violet.' But he looked pleased that Felix was now settled in his arm. With the other he hugged her, lightly.

'My beloved family,' he said.

She relaxed into him, the memory of the insects fading. She felt tired though, as if she had seen something she shouldn't have, and now had to keep the reality of it secret.

That night, as Archie made love to her, tenderly caressing her back and breasts, she felt as if his hands were like insects crawling over her and had to hold her breath to stifle a desire to scream out loud with repulsion. She endured his hard thrusting, waiting for the ordeal to be over. Oblivious to her imaginings, Archie then quickly fell asleep. Restless, she crept out of the bed and into the bathroom. Taking a bath, she soaped herself, still feeling the traces of the insects on her skin. She dried herself quickly, enjoying the dry roughness of the coarse cotton towel. Quietly she crept back into bed and manoeuvred herself to the side so they were no longer touching.

When Violet woke up, Archie had already got up and left for London. He knew that the servants would be present in the house and their lovemaking must have reassured him that she had recovered. She couldn't hear Felix and went through to the nursery that was next to their bedroom. He was fast asleep in his nightgown, his fingers up against his cheek as if he were deep in thought. She resisted picking Felix up, holding his soft sweet-scented body to her and never letting it go. Wasn't it supposed to be a sin to wake up a sleeping baby? How beautiful he was, she thought. She gently traced the outline of his round cheek with the tip of her finger. His eyelashes fluttered, but remained shut. Her baby was perfect. There was nothing wrong with him.

But was there something wrong with her? Should she tell a doctor perhaps what she had seen? But the delusion seemed so strange, so out of the ordinary that she felt she could exclude it from her real life. Lock the image away in a box, so that it no longer had anything to do with her. The insects had been a strange illusion brought about by the sleepless nights, the exhaustion of the birth. Perhaps she should think about hiring a nanny as Archie had suggested. But the idea of handing over the care of Felix to someone else was anathema to her.

She would forget about the delusion. The birds were singing outside. It was a lovely day. She would get dressed and take

Felix for a walk in his pram around the estate. She would be his guardian, protect and care and love him. This motherly love lay deep within her, a fact now of her life, just as Felix was now a fact of her life. She was the luckiest woman alive and all traces of the memory of those abominable crawling insects had vanished.

Chapter 10

Violet hid all the knives away.

'Where are the knives, darling?' Archie asked.

'They're blunt. They need sharpening,' she said.

But one had cut her finger deeply as she passed it over her skin before putting it in the back of a drawer. Its blade had been so sharp. It had shone, the steel, in the moonlight. The night was silent. She had wanted to check the sharpness of the blade, out of curiosity. So she had carefully wrapped the knives up in kitchen cloths and put them at the back of a drawer they never used.

When they didn't reappear, Archie asked the housekeeper to order new ones. Violet felt she couldn't hide the new knives, so she tried not to look at them whenever she saw them lying out.

She went into the village to post some letters. Mrs Hutchinson was talking to the girl behind the counter at the Post Office. Mrs Hutchinson's blue eyes were dancing with excitement. 'It's not like Amy to disappear without a trace. Such a shy girl.' Mrs Hutchinson lived in a cottage at the far end of the village. Her grey hair was escaping from thick plaits that were tied up around her head like a laurel crown.

'It's not, and she had just been released too,' replied the girl behind the counter. 'Her mother is distraught. '

'So she should be. She should have kept more of an eye on her. It's always the quiet ones.'

'So you think she ran off?'

'What else could it be?'

'*I* heard she had just started seeing Patrick Harper.'

Mrs Hutchinson didn't reply. She didn't like being disagreed with, especially if her opinions were based on hearsay rather than fact. The shakier the ground the more determined and affronted she became. Violet remembered Amy as quiet too. She had once seen her ambling lethargically up the street pulling the lead on her dog, who seemed even more relaxed than she was. Her body was shapely and she had walked with a kind of stooping, elaborate, slow grace.

'Had her mother noticed anything odd?' Mrs Hutchinson asked.

'Amy was always odd!'

The two women laughed, heartlessly.

'Why was she odd?' Violet couldn't help asking.

Mrs Hutchinson and the girl turned towards her simultaneously, as if they had only just noticed she was in the shop with them. She hadn't been hiding, Violet thought. They looked startled to see her. More startled than by the unexplained disappearance of Amy Louden.

'She would mutter to herself. Quotes,' the girl said.

'From where?' Violet asked.

'Fairy tales, I think. They were quotations about love.'

Life seemed evasive. Violet had created an astringent limbo land for herself of reading and watching instead of living, only brought alive by the gaze of others. Her own perception of herself was not strong or certain enough to give herself credence.

Her friend Bea said, 'It's dangerous, your small enclosed world – it doesn't exist.'

'Yes, it does. It's my reality.'

'But only in a cocoon.'

'I'm managing.'

But she felt at the heart a kind of fear at what was happening, how she had put all her power into Archie's hands, how naturally and inevitably it had happened.

Why was it, she wondered, that she disappeared so easily? She was like Tinkerbell who needed applause in order to stay alive.

When she looked down at her body she could see that she was real but how often now did she feel disconnected from her body, having lost herself in the ether of her mind? And her body was her only connection with the material world, the flesh and bone of it.

At the time, she was not fully conscious of what was happening to her, fears growing up around her like jungle plants, suffocating her energy. She hardly knew why she kept crying. It was just a feeling of terrible loss that this baby was beginning to signify, that she was losing Archie all because of the baby and that she would never get him back. All because of the baby, that soft, succulent creature of rosy flesh and open sweet blood-red mouth wanting her milk.

She started not to want to touch Felix, that soft skin that she had once loved to touch. His warm flesh felt repulsive, made her feel uneasy, as if the surface of him was invading the surface of her skin. She could only tolerate him when he was fully clothed. She started to visualise peeling off the skin, leaving him raw and red, as if in some way that would reduce the power he had over her.

Devastating anguish followed these fantasies. It was as if the violent imagery of her thoughts had become detached from her true self, a rational link severed, so that these images came grasping and unbidden to her mind. She felt they were nothing to do with her and as such she was not responsible for them. No one need know about them. After all, it was not as if she were really going to act upon them, do what they were suggesting her to do. They had no power over her as long as she kept strong and resistant to them.

CHAPTER 11

HER THOUGHTS KEPT returning obsessively to the book of fairy tales. She knew there was a clue in there somewhere to what was happening to her mind. When Archie was out of the house, she returned to his study, took down the painting and opened the safe again. She took out the book and looked at the first letters of the chapters, the last letters, combed it for possible anagrams, diagonal messages. She could find no pattern. She looked at the pictures. The mermaid in the sea. The girl dancing in the red shoes. The wild swans flying in formation. No little strange details in the pictures. What was so special about this book? She flicked through the stories again. All stories she had read as a child and didn't need to read again. She put the book away. She noticed the cream circle on the green cover had been filled in a little to look like a waxing moon.

That night she dreamt of a naked corpse hanging in a room of dark rock, arms and legs pulled apart in a triangle, an image from the anatomy book she had been reading. The skin had been peeled off to reveal the bloodied flesh of the body, the veins, the muscles. Flies hovered in the air. Discarded strips of skin lay around on the floor. She tried not to retch as she bent over on the floor, the hem of her dress becoming soaked in blood, her pale satin pumps now soiled red in a lacy filigree.

She woke up next to Archie, screaming. He quickly turned

on the gaslight and tried to calm her. She garbled her dream to him in detail, hysterically.

He went white. 'I'm calling the doctor.'

'No,' she shouted. 'No, I don't need a doctor.'

She struggled.

'No, I'm not ill. I'm fine.' But the doctor arrived and she noticed that his face was a blank. There were no features on his face at all, just a cowl of skin where his face should have been. The doctor manhandled her onto the bed and rolled up her sleeve.

'What is it?'

'Something that will calm you down.'

Morphine, she thought. They are giving me morphine. And a few moments after the injection had been given she felt nothing was more important than anything else. She could hear Felix crying in the background and it sounded like the harmless mewing of a cat.

As she lay on the bed, she heard her doctor say to Archie:

'We'll need you to sign the certificate.'

'You think this is necessary?'

'Yes. It's a form of hysteria that's been brought about by the birth of her baby. It is rare but I have known of previous cases. You say she is having extremely violent nightmares? And, more significantly, delusions about your son?'

Archie nodded. 'What will happen to her?'

'It means we have to look after her. And then she can come back home.'

'I only want what is best for her.'

'It is the only way. Unless you wish to have her looked after at home. But she is clearly a danger not only to Felix but herself.'

'I only want her to be well again.'

'Then sign here.'

Violet heard, after the rustle of documents being brought out, the sound of the scratch of the pen on the document. In a vacant state she watched Archie packing some of her clothes in a suitcase, her green velvet dress, underclothes, dressing gown, slippers, toilet bag. It was like she was looking at the distant horizon of a flat sea, beneath a steel-grey sky.

The doctor, still with his featureless face, brought her unsteadily to her feet. Archie dressed her in front of the doctor. She felt no shame, just a mild curiosity as to what the doctor must be thinking at her husband's strange behaviour.

They led her to the carriage.

Archie gently settled her in, then leapt out again, before she could grab hold of him, and shut the door.

She said through the open window, 'You're not coming? I want you to come.'

'You know I can't. I have to look after Felix.'

'Oh yes, of course.' She had forgotten all about Felix.

'Make sure they look after her well, there,' Archie said to the doctor.

'Of course. I know all the doctors who work there, personally.'

Archie gave Violet one of his most sincere smiles as the carriage set off. She was amazed at how Archie was dealing with this crisis with such equanimity. She looked out of the carriage window. It was growing dark. She was surprised at how late it had become. She could see the sun going down behind the black silhouettes of the trees. The carriage set off down the driveway, the rattling oddly comforting. She felt strangely relieved to be leaving behind her previous life.

CHAPTER 12

THE CARRIAGE DROVE swiftly until they reached the asylum. It was a large Victorian building, heavy and imposing. The carriage drew up in front of the impressive entrance flanked by colonnades and the doctor helped Violet out and up the wide grey stone steps. She was beginning to feel oddly elated. As if this place was just a new version of her old home.

The doctor led her into the huge entrance hall and down a gas-lit dingy white corridor and up some back stairs. She could hear women shouting from behind closed doors but she could see no one. The place seemed completely empty. There was an institutional smell of bleach and damp. There was another scream. The doctor took her into a small bare room with a narrow bed taking up most of the space.

'Someone will come for you in the morning, Lady Murray, to settle you in.'

He shut the door and she heard the lock turn. She undressed unsteadily, washed in the basin in the corner of the room and gingerly climbed into bed. Her mind felt dazed and incoherent. A music hall song kept on going around in her head.

She felt the bed was floating like a boat on water. Her stomach felt light. The light-headedness was delicious after all the anxiety and fretting of the past few months. What on earth had she been worrying about? Then she remembered

Felix. What a lovely baby he was, how healthy and strong. He was so fine with or without her. She felt relieved to be in this lovely new self-contained room. She didn't have to worry about anything any more. She could give over her life, without guilt or regret.

In the morning the novelty had worn off, and her enthusiasm was dissipating. She now felt mildly curious and wondered how long she was going to have to stay here. Her body ached where she had been manhandled. In the asylum there were no places to hide and she was exposed in all ways. They had taken her clothes in the night and dressed her in a loose-fitting gown of serge cotton. The material gaped open, and her flesh was on view unless she held her gown tightly around her. There was nowhere to hide the expression on her face. She imagined the gaslight in the room would show all the structure of her cheekbones, the fine lines on her forehead and around her eyes. Even the shadows beneath her eyes would be emphasised by the obliquity of the light.

A new doctor walked in. He had a face, a face with strong features that seemed to dictate the world around him. He was middle-aged and handsome with flecks of grey in his dark hair. He exuded a strong commanding aura as if he had been hewn from the asylum's stone. He put her immediately at ease. He seemed eminently reasonable. She could smell the pungent scent of sweat on him – it was not unattractive. She was feeling oddly sensual. Was it the morphine, the delusions, her heightened awareness? He seemed to pick up on this, seemed vaguely amused and unaffected. But she wondered if he was truly unaffected. She wondered if when men appeared to grow calm, they were actually trying to contain attraction for someone.

She noticed when he grasped her wrist to take her pulse that he had hairs on the back of his hand and his arm like a werewolf. He was so different from Archie, who was so lithe and slim and hairless. Archie could disappear.

'How are you feeling, Lady Murray?'

She felt odd, exuberant, tired, sexual, alert, oblivious, all at the same time. How could she explain?

'Distracted?' he continued.

'A little.'

'That is normal. You are still under the influence of the morphine.'

He had a German accent.

'When will I be allowed home?'

He laughed loudly. 'But you have only just come to us.'

'So how long will I be here?' She felt persistent.

'However long it takes for you to recover.'

'How long will that be?'

'That I cannot tell. The delusions have to stop first.'

'I haven't had any since I've arrived.'

'That's good. Very good. How many were you having previously?'

'It just happened once.'

'And nightmares?'

'Just once.'

He wrote this down. She didn't like him writing this down. She couldn't be sure of the exact facts any more. Not sure at all.

'Approximately,' she added.

But he didn't write this down.

'And did the delusion involve your baby?'

'Yes.'

'And the nightmare. Who did that involve?'

She thought of the hanging corpse. 'Me.'

'What do you mean?'

'It involved skin.'

'Can you be more specific?'

She shook her head.

He was writing frantically now.

'Sounds like projections. Projections of your own trauma. The trauma of childbirth.'

'But the childbirth was normal.'

He looked at her strangely, as if she were lying to him.

She was still wounded from the birth, still ashamed at how she had been ripped open. She had bled after the birth so much it had coated the sheets.

The doctor's lips were beginning to part. Her heart raced. Oh no. He was giving a smile. *Don't, please don't.* His lips pulled back to reveal a strong set of perfect teeth. She was still looking at him, trying to seem calm.

She made to rise from the bed but he quickly took her legs firmly and gently and put them back under the covers.

'You need bed rest, Lady Murray.'

'There is nothing for me to do here.'

'Did you bring any books?'

'No.'

'I will see what I can find for you.'

It was only that afternoon, after she had been lying in bed for hours, mindlessly looking at the ceiling, that he finally brought her some books. They were history books.

'No novels,' she observed.

'We don't think novels are helpful for the mind of an ill patient. They can over-excite.'

How right he was. She opened up a history of Napoleon and started reading about his military campaigns.

A nurse came in and left some flowers in a vase.

'These are from your husband.'

They were her favourite, tulips.

'Does he not want to visit me?'

'You're not allowed visitors yet, Lady Murray.'

'Oh.'

The nurse brought in supper, soup and fruit salad, but still they would not allow her out of her room. She could just see sky and the top of a tree's branches outside the asylum window. She wanted to get back to Felix. She felt restless and guilty. Her breasts leaked with milk. Her breasts seemed so full and heavy and she had to pump the milk away, tears streaming down her face, and then watch as a nurse poured the milk down the sink. She washed before going to bed where she had a sleepless night in which she could hear Felix crying for her.

The next morning, the doctor returned.

'My baby needs me,' she said.

'He is being well looked after.'

'How do you know?' His kindness was beginning to irk her; she was feeling it was false.

'Your husband is a considerate man. Did he not send you flowers?'

She didn't say anything. Archie had worked his spell on the doctor, too, she thought. He came across as the loving, caring husband, so proud of his wife and son, but he didn't really care.

He would say how proud he was of his family, but why, she thought, didn't she feel any of his love? She saw the appearance of love. What was missing in him? Or was it what was really missing in her?

'He talks about you very fondly.'

'Yes.'

She could see the doctor thinking that she should be grateful.

'Don't worry, your son is fine. But we don't want the delusions to come back.'

'I'm fine. I promise. I need to get home.' Tears, in spite of herself, were filling her eyes.

'You are working yourself up needlessly, Lady Murray. You need to relax. You don't want to harm your baby again, do you?'

'I haven't harmed him.'

The doctor looked surprised. 'Don't you remember?'

'Remember what?'

He started writing in his book.

'What do you mean, I don't remember? Are you saying I harmed my baby? Did Archie tell you about the scratches? It was only my fingernails. Because of the insects.'

The panic was starting up. She was feeling hysterical.

'Don't go. I need an explanation.'

'Lady Murray. You're tired. Everything is fine. You need to sleep.'

CHAPTER 13

S HE STOOD UP to look out of the small window. Through the bars, she saw the mottled leaves of the tree and the silhouette of a bird perched on a branch. She thought the bird was part of the tree before it fluttered to a lower branch, vivid and alive like a panicked thought. She thought of home, of Archie and her baby and the garden. I will be with them soon, she thought. They will be waiting for me in the garden with the rhododendron and the rosemary and the scent of lavender and the hot sun beating down. And she crawled onto her bed and put the coarse blanket over her head and fell into a dark place where nothing, no memories or longing, could reach her, just a deathless present.

In her memory, Archie was even more handsome and strong. He began to represent all the strength that she had lost in here, all her hope for future happiness. She had to remind herself he had only put her in here out of concern for her welfare and a desire to protect Felix. He had had no choice. Any angry thoughts were quickly subsumed by gratitude. Who knows what might have happened, what she might have done to Felix if Archie had not taken this course? This place was a cure for her dreadful imagination. And once she realised that, she moved towards acceptance of her situation. She learned to wait, for if it were a justifiable punishment, it would be finite. At some point this would all come to an end.

For the next few days she just slept and ate, seeing only the nurse who bustled in and out to change the sheets or bring her food. The screams of the other patients became background noise, ceasing to have any effect on her. After a while she stopped thinking about Felix. He only appeared in her dreams, looking up at her in her arms, with his dark eyes, seeing everything that was necessary, no more and no less.

The only colours in the room were the latest flowers her husband had sent her. She stared at them, the lush purple and sensual pink of the poppies with the morass of seething blackness at their centre. She would stare at them for hours, as if the colour could bleed into her, bring her back to life.

The doctor came in.

'Have any of the delusions come back?

'No.'

'None at all?'

'No.'

She watched, waiting for the doctor to smile, in case he was just another delusion. This time the doctor didn't smile. 'We will be able perhaps to reduce your medication.'

'Thank you.'

'You don't seem very pleased.'

She just shrugged her shoulders.

'You will still need to stay in a while longer. For observation. To see how you do under the lesser dose.'

He disappeared suddenly. And a moment later she saw him in an adjoining room through a glass window laughing with Archie, saw the doctor being charmed. But Archie turned towards her and she saw it was not Archie after all, but someone she had never seen before.

Violet was allowed out of her room in the early mornings to clean the asylum floors. The corridor floor was so shiny and polished she had to walk carefully in case she slipped.

Some of the doors to the rooms were open, others were shut. She looked into one room and saw that grey rubber lined the walls and floor.

She washed the ward floor for the third time that day. The soapy water splashed up and over the white tiles. She also cleaned the walls that were opposite the lavatory stalls, which had no doors. A nurse like a little Dutch doll with short blonde hair and pearly blue eyes painted onto an oval face came to supervise her. She looked innocuous but every so often a look of malice entered her eyes. She wants to manipulate me, Violet thought.

'The floor is still dirty. You will need to do it again,' the nurse said quietly.

Violet picked up the bucket and poured the dirty water over the nurse's head. The nurse gave a smile through the water dripping from her cap and face, as if this was what she had been waiting for all along,

'It's the rubber room for you,' she said and dragged Violet along the corridor and flung her into the well-padded grey room.

After the nurse had locked the door behind her, Violet stood still for a moment before beginning to throw herself against the wall repeatedly, not sure whether this room was real or just part of a dream where there would be no consequences. A place where she could jump off the edge of a precipitous cliff and land in a cushion of marsh-cotton flowers. Finally exhausted, she curled up in a corner of the room and fell asleep. She woke up to the sound of the door being opened by the nurse.

'Violet,' the nurse said commandingly.

She turned round again. Was that her name? She saw the nurse had in her hand a plate of boiled beef and potatoes. She placed it down on the floor by Violet's mattress.

'You need to eat this. You're looking thin.'

Violet looked down at her long arms. Her skin looked so translucent she could see through it to the veins and blood and muscles, as if her arm were an anatomy drawing.

'How long have I been here?'

'You really don't remember?'

Violet shook her head. She could see the nurse make a note of this in her head and Violet inwardly cursed herself. She had to be careful. If she wanted to get out of this place she had to be careful, like a pierrot clown tip-toeing along a plank in a circus, a few feet above the ground. This place was full of disturbed people; it was a place that succumbed to psychotic things.

'A few days?' she guessed, uncertainly for she had lost so much weight.

'You have been here lying comatose for a long time. Delirious. You kept saying Felix, Felix, over and over.'

'He's my son.'

'I know.' And then the nurse's head rotated right round.

Violet tried to keep her face impassive, not register her horror.

The nurse continued as if nothing out of the ordinary had happened.

'It's important you eat. Or you know what we have to do.'

Violet didn't know, but she sat down on the mattress, balancing the plate precariously on her knees, and skewered a piece of meat and put it in her mouth. She chewed and chewed. She knew she would find it difficult to swallow, and when she tried she started to choke. The chewed meat spewed out of her mouth, back on to the plate.

'I'm sorry. I can't.'

The nurse had watched her intently. She picked up the plate with a disapproving manner.

'I am going to have to call the doctor,' she said.

Violet nodded. She remembered the doctor. He had been kind. He would help her get her out of here.

'Where is Felix?' she asked.

'Best not to talk about him now. It will only upset you.'

Tears had started to pour down Violet's face. Where are they coming from, she wondered. All this water inside her, pouring out of her eyes. If felt so strange. But she needed to know about Felix. And there was something in the harsh tone of the nurse that made her think, he is better off without me. He is being well looked after now.

CHAPTER 14

THE DOCTOR AND the doll-nurse came into the padded room. The force-feeding equipment, with its narrow rubber tube, was coiled up like a sleeping snake in the nurse's arms. The nurse forced the rubber tube up Violet's nostrils as she struggled. The fluid gushed up her nose, down her throat into her stomach. As she tried to resist, the doctor held her down. The pain and discomfort were so great she wanted to scream, but she thought, I must remain quiet so I can get back to Felix.

The next day she heard the handle of the door turn and the doctor came in. He looked the same but she felt different, as if she had once been in the same world and now had been exiled to this different world for those who had strange dreams.

'Hello, Lady Murray,' he said. He was looking at her in exactly the same way he had always done. There was no shock or pity in his eyes but she knew this was his professional manner. She knew exactly what she looked like. She had seen her face reflected in the blunt knives they gave her to eat with. Her eyes were staring with an odd light, as if she had seen visions. Her hair was tied harshly back. Her sagging skin had grown dry.

'You are prepared to start eating again?'

'Yes,' she said.

He made notes with his pen. His handwriting was slanted

and regular. The writing, she thought, of a man in control of everything: emotions, his life and other peoples' lives. By fate and circumstance he had become entitled to wield power.

'How is Felix?' she asked.

He wrote for a while longer, then looked up.

'We don't think it's good for your recovery to discuss that. You can return to your room now. It's dinnertime.'

Dinner was the only time when all the other inmates came together. They congregated in the dining hall, a large cavernous dark, institutional room, lined by wood panelling with rows of tables and benches. A large oil portrait of the founder of the asylum, a man with a grey beard and apparently benign eyes, hung above the head table where the doctors and staff ate.

As Violet struggled to eat her meal of meat and potatoes and gravy, a plump young woman sat down opposite her. Violet was used to eating alone and looked up, resentfully. The woman had black curly hair, olive skin and pugnacious features. She seemed lively and different from the other thin, passive women in the asylum who haunted the place like ghosts. Violet wondered what she was doing here.

'You'll get used to it here, dear. Don't cause trouble with the nurses. Just do what they say. And pretend. Pretend to be normal. Then you get out sooner. I'm Betsy.' Her bizarrely optimistic face beamed at her with rosy cheeks. Round her neck she wore a silver pendant in the form of a letter B. 'They use threats here. Threats that unless you do what they say, you will never be able to leave. That's how they keep you down! You have to get better in spite of them. Use your own will. Shrewdness. And fire.' She laughed gaily.

It was the first authentic conversation Violet felt she had had in weeks. It was as if she were listening to the truth directly rather than trying to overhear it through a dense fog.

'Are you going to be let out soon?'

Betsy smiled. 'Oh, I'm never going to be let out.'

'But you seem perfectly sane.'

'Oh, I am. But my husband wants me in here. He pays the owner of the asylum to keep me here. He has moved his mistress into our house. She has become the mother to my children.'

She said this with vivacity, with a happy gleam in her eye.

And Violet suddenly wondered about her sanity, after all.

'But don't you worry about me. We all have our problems in here. Look after yourself first. Do what I say. And play the game. It is all just a game here. Everyone is pretending to cope, the mad with their madness, the nurses with their impossible jobs, the doctors with their new-fangled cures.'

Violet looked around the room. Women were eating or staring into space, or looking into the fire or wandering aimlessly around the room. And for an insane moment she thought, this is no different from normality, just women existing and surviving, this is what happens to women who don't fit into a world created by men.

CHAPTER 15

A FEW DAYS later, she was walking down one of the corridors when, in the flickering gaslight, she saw a tall man with the natural fluidity of Archie moving down the passageway and then turning left into the hallway.

'Archie,' she shouted. She ran after him, her legs getting caught in her long nightdress, forcing her to take smaller steps. 'Archie, wait. It's me.' The man didn't look round but turned the corner out of sight. He was leaving the building without her. A hand forcefully grasped her arm.

She turned round to see the doctor's strong assured face. He looked as if he were about to lean over and kiss her, he looked possessed. She bent back from him as far as she could, instinctively. He was still holding her arm so tightly it was hurting. The beard had more flecks of grey than before, she could see that. Had so much time passed? Or had she just never seen his face so close up to her before?

'Archie, it was Archie,' she said in a quick whisper. 'You saw him, didn't you? Has he come to take me away?'

'Calm down,' he said. But it was he who looked harried. He's been caught out, she thought, he doesn't like that. He has been seeing my husband behind my back and not telling me. And she remembered Archie's secret walks at night, his previous walks to the edge of the asylum's estate.

'What have you been saying to him?' she asked. 'You've been saying I'm not ready to leave, haven't you?'

He looked at her gently, but came out with the cruellest of words.

'Quite the opposite, Lady Murray,' he said.

She was too bewildered to question him further as he gently led her back to her room. All her bones ached as she lay down on the bed and flung the grey blanket over her.

What did he mean, she wondered over and over again, by 'quite the opposite'? She couldn't work it out. The words seemed so muddled in her head she couldn't connect them with a meaning. Archie would never have left her here if he had been sure she was ready to leave. He would want her home with him. And with Felix. He would want his family together. She knew that about him. How important she was to him, how important his family was, how he would do everything to keep his beloved family together.

Over the following week, as her mind gradually became more lucid, she began to see the asylum not as a collection of misguided rules but a collective organisation run to carefully laid-out regulations, involving systematic observance of the inmates' behaviour. This of course was subject to the individual jailor's idiosyncrasy, his or her power-hungry whims or sadistic impulses.

The head of the asylum or his lackeys could manipulate the rules for their own ambitions and lack of empathy was key to furthering their own ends. Any weakness or sign of madness was a sign of their failure. It was a perfect combination and she thought of organised responsibility and individual temperament. The doctors, as well as the inmates, were highly confined in their own small world where madness was managed by systematising it and difference eradicated by using medical treatments. It had become about method, not result.

She longed to return to the unassisted loneliness of her marriage but something in the back of her mind had begun to disturb her. Was there a hidden system to her marriage she hadn't realised, also? Was she no less manipulated in her marriage than she was here? But she put this to the back of her mind. The only thing wrong with her marriage was herself and her delusions. It was her madness that manipulated her, no one or nothing else.

The doctor came into her room. 'A few more days and you will be able to leave,' he said. He told her she would be allowed to wear her own nightgown. She saw his grey beard, his lively intelligent eyes, his genuine smile. He seemed so unthreatening and she felt so grateful.

She would be let out soon, she thought, to see Felix. She tried to separate him from her life here, didn't want him to be tainted by this place, even in her memory. If she thought about him here, he would be associated with this place, but she couldn't help but think of him. The memory of him would drift towards her. She wondered how he had changed, how Archie and he had managed without her. Oh, she hoped Archie hadn't altered their way of life too much. She wanted everything to be exactly the same when she returned, as if she had never been away.

CHAPTER 16

'HERE, LET ME help you.' The asylum doctor pulled back the bed sheets. She felt naked, although her own nightgown covered her amply, flowing around her like a bridal gown, lace trimmed. He took her hand and pulled her gently to her feet. 'Here, I'll take you to the drawing room.'

She moved hesitantly down the corridor, her legs weak. He took her into a dark room, with paintings hanging on the red and gold flock wallpaper, and china ornaments standing forlornly in glass cabinets. There was a smell in the room, of lilies and death. An oppressive aura that permeated the rich mahogany furniture and golden-framed paintings of the previous doctors who had worked in the asylum. It was a facsimile of a drawing room in a country house.

'This room is for our special patients, who are soon ready to leave.'

By special she presumed he meant wealthy.

'Stay here a little. Read. Look out into the garden.' He then brought out a book from his pocket wrapped in pale blue tissue paper.

'Archie has brought you this.'

She tore off the tissue paper. It was a beautiful calf-bound book. The pages were blank.

'Looks like human skin, doesn't it?' the doctor said.

Violet held it tenderly in her hands, stroked the softness.

She opened it up. Archie had inscribed it inside. '*To a new beginning.*' She felt an urgent need to get back to her husband and son, to feel safe again.

She glanced out into the garden. Beech hedges crisscrossed the formal layout of beddings and gravel paths, stretching out to the woodlands at the end. Beyond that lay the rest of the uncultivated estate that bordered the road that led to their own estate. Everything here was so ordered, she thought. And in this dark, heavy, still room, also silent. The doctor put his hand on her shoulder and left it there for a moment as if in a medical benediction. He then closed the heavy dark wooden door behind him. She sat down on the leather armchair by the window. She felt oddly self-conscious as if someone was staring at her.

A while later, a nurse wheeled in an old woman in a wheelchair. The nurse bustled about her, warm and kind yet patronising, as if she knew all the questions you were going to ask and had an answer for them all. Giving endlessly of herself, in spite of her short stature, as there was so much of her to give. The old woman's head was bowed over, as if not conscious but not asleep either, as if in no-man's land. It frightened Violet deeply to see that inward state of being. The nurse wheeled the old woman to the window and left the room again. The woman's head remained bowed, and Violet noticed a small burn mark on each of the woman's temples, as if she had been kissed by fire, twice.

Violet watched dust motes hover in the air. It was stuffy. She thought about opening the window but saw that it was locked – to stop people getting in or out, she wondered? The door opened again and she turned to see a young woman, also in her own nightgown, enter. She had long auburn hair, and a little retroussé nose.

'Do you mind if I join you?' She had a rough accent, and

Violet wondered why someone from her background was in this room. Violet's own background had been painted over.

'Not at all.' But Violet did not feel like the company of others, felt too shy and withdrawn. It would be an effort to seem normal. However, the woman seemed to feel the same way. She sat down in the chair opposite and stared out the window.

Finally, she turned her head to face Violet and stared at her unflinchingly.

'I'm Donna.'

'Violet.'

'What are you in here for?'

'You make it sounds like we're criminals.'

'Isn't that what we are? Our crime is not to fit in.'

'They are here to help us!'

'Are you so sure?' Donna gave a sharp smile. 'It's more like to help everyone else. To make their lives easier.'

'I've not felt normal since the birth of my son.'

'Ah.'

'I became very anxious. I started to see things crawling on my baby.'

'I see.'

Donna laughed again, a bitter little laugh, more like a gasp of pain.

'I have visions, too. But of a better world.'

She was very pretty, Violet thought, and Donna's anger gave her an unusual edge.

'Will you play chess with me?' Donna asked.

Violet said, 'I don't play very often.'

'It will pass the time.'

But it only passed a little time as Donna beat her swiftly.

'I forked you like a snake's tongue.'

Violet noticed a small scar like a snakeskin running down her leg. Donna saw her looking at it.

'It's from dancing. I fell off the stage, once.'

How much of this was true, Violet wondered?

'You're Lady Murray, aren't you?'

She nodded.

'I've seen your husband. He comes here at night sometimes.'

'To try and see me?'

'No, before you arrived here. Since the start of the year.'

'What do you mean?' No, she didn't want to think this was true.

'I see him talking to the doctor. Your husband pays him. I've seen him hand him over money.'

'Pays him for what?'

Donna shrugged her shoulders. 'Who knows? Who cares?'

'I care.'

Donna grimaced, tried to reassure her. 'Don't worry, love. It's all harmless.'

The short nurse came back in.

'Donna. It's your turn for treatment.'

Donna stood up. 'Hope I don't end up like that!' And she nodded in the direction of the trance-like woman in the wheelchair at the window. 'They burn your thoughts with electricity. But they'll sort me out. You'll see.' She gave a bitter laugh. She leant forward and shook Violet's hand.

Violet heard the door close again behind Donna and the nurse. She felt uneasy.

The doctor returned. 'You are ready to go home now.' They took her back to her room, and gave her back her suitcase of clothes. She was trembling with excitement as she laced her corset and pulled her heavy green velvet dress over it. She pinched her wan cheeks to give them colour. She wanted to look as she had when Archie had first met her.

By dusk the carriage was driving down their drive. She saw the manor house at the end of it. She had forgotten how elegant their home was, how delicate the architecture, compared to the heavy frontage of the asylum. How reassuring it was to be finally home, and she couldn't wait to see Felix again.

CHAPTER 17

STANDING AT THE top of the entrance steps of their house, waiting for her, was a woman Violet had never seen before. She was fair and pretty like a fairy tale princess or ballerina. In her arms she was holding Felix. In that moment, Violet thought, she looked like the mistress of the house, with the heir in her arms, but as she grew closer, she could see that her clothes, although perfectly presentable, were slightly worn. As Violet alighted from the carriage, Archie was nowhere to be seen.

The woman came down the steps to greet her. She was like a still pond. Her thin fair hair fell in strands onto her shoulders like spun gold. She smiled slowly, as if a shadow of a cloud was slowly lifting from a field.

'I'm Clara.'

Violet reached out to take Felix in her arms and Clara immediately handed him over to her. He was fast asleep. His long black eyelashes were long, curled up against his cheek. His soft rosebud mouth was slightly pursed. Violet placed a finger gently on his palm and his fingers curled round her own.

A feeling of maternal love swept over Violet that was so powerful it made her feel faint. Noticing this, the new nanny stepped in quickly and took Felix from her arms, so naturally, Violet thought.

'It's bed time,' Clara said firmly as Felix stirred and Violet watched as his head nestled into her neck.

'Good night, Felix,' Violet said. Softly, too softly, frightened of disturbing the boy. But he didn't turn his head as Clara climbed back up the steps and disappeared into the house with him.

At last, Archie came running out of the front door onto the gravel driveway to meet her and flung his strong arms around her.

'Welcome home, my darling.'

'I'm so happy to be back,' she said, tears in her eyes, tears of gratitude that she had been cured. She was so relieved to be surrounded by loving people and that Felix had been so well cared for. And she would be able to be a good mother to Felix now that she was cured.

That night, at dinner, she looked at Archie's face in the candlelight, surreptitiously as she didn't want to seem over-curious to him. He did look different, she thought, harder round the edges, his gestures heavier. They ate their first course in silence. As they waited for their plates to be cleared, she suddenly asked, 'Did you miss me, Archie? I missed you. And Felix of course.'

He was looking at her as if for the first time, as if he had only just noticed her.

'Of course I did, darling.' He smiled his generous smile. 'But I knew it had to be done for your sake. For all our sakes.'

'Of course.' She looked down at the white tablecloth. A breeze from the open window caressed her bare arms, made her silk dress flutter like a moth's wing. She tried to concentrate on remaining sitting on the chair. She was scared she might fly away, if she made a quick insubstantial movement. She started to play with a fork, its silver glimmering in the candlelight.

'Felix seems so well.'

'Clara has done such a good job.'

'Yes.'

She looked at his narrow strong shoulders, his perfect shape in its dinner jacket. He was like a shiny toy soldier, she thought, made of tin.

'It's going to take a while for you to fully recover, darling,' Archie said.

But there was no sympathy in his eyes, she thought, only that new brittleness. Or was it new? Was it just that she hadn't noticed it before? She wanted to rush round to him, hold him, grasp the old Archie, the one she had loved so intensely, but her hands were gripping the chair too tightly, afraid that she would slip away into the ether.

That night they made love. He was tender, insidious, reassuring. She felt protected, loved, drained. He touched her in a way he had not before, as if he knew her better than she knew herself. Afterwards, she heard him fall quickly into sleep. She lay awake, luxuriating in the soft cotton sheets against her skin, the scent of lavender emanating from the open window. She looked up at the white corniced ceiling with its intricate swirls, like icing on a wedding cake.

How she longed for normality, to be how she had been before the birth, to regain that innocence before the madness had struck her and given her such a terrible knowledge it was now impossible to lose. She did not know what the knowledge consisted of. She only knew it had a heavy darkness at its centre, like the poppy head, bowing low.

She fell into a fitful sleep where she was walking through a field of white poppies with their dark centre and petals outlined in a black inky line, unable to find a way out, surrounded by the intense scent of her new knowledge.

Such was Clara's strange presence, Violet felt, unless she resisted, she would be engulfed in it: there was no edge to her, she was full of curves. She was amorphous. Her big blue slowly blinking eyes were like discs of wonder, as if Clara couldn't quite believe in her own existence, as if she was her very own constant surprise.

Bea, when she came round to visit, was clearly impressed by Clara's competent manner. When she and Violet were alone, Bea asked if Clara was seeing anyone.

'I don't think so,' Violet said, surprised at the question.

'I think we need to find Clara a nice young man. I know just the person.'

'Who?'

'My nephew. He's coming to stay with us for a few months. He interested in farming and he needs a wife who knows the value of hard work. Not some upper crust lady who doesn't want to soil her hands. Clara is wonderful with Felix.'

'Yes.'

'And she'll make a wonderful mother. A good wife. And most importantly of all, as far as Ralph goes, she's beautiful.'

Violet mentioned this to Archie, that night.

'Bea and I are going to try to matchmake Clara.'

'Oh? Are you sure that's a good idea? We might lose her.'

'I hadn't thought of that. But it will be fine. He's local.'

'And who's the lucky gentleman?'

'Bea's nephew Ralph.'

'Well, I don't think he'll have much luck!'

'Why not?'

'Because Clara doesn't strike me as the marrying kind.'

She was astonished. How on earth did Archie know that? He never noticed anything, as he rooted obliviously around in his own masculine world. He noticed her surprised expression.

'Oh, I can just tell. She's kind of shut off,' he continued.

'Well, we'll see. Ralph sounds like a rather fine man.'

Archie stood up from the table. 'Well, I think it's a stupid idea and will end in trouble.'

'Don't be so pessimistic, Archie. It's not like you.'

Archie turned round and snapped at her – 'And don't you be so interfering' – and stormed out of the room. He seemed so irritable, she thought. When they had first met he had been so attentive. Which was the real version, she wondered? She longed for the return of the original version, as if Archie had been replaced by an imposter. She gave up on the idea of finding someone for Clara.

CHAPTER 18

CLARA WAS AN expert at everything she did. She helped the maidservants with the cleaning, cared for Felix, and agreed with all of Violet's opinions as if they were her own. Felix always appeared in the morning rested, dressed in his smart clean baby clothes. Violet was still not well enough to attend to his practical needs but she could read, and take walks in the garden as Clara and Felix played together, and she was content to relinquish the care of him. Clara would show him pictures in a book, carry him around the garden, and pick flowers for him to smell.

Violet noticed how devoted Felix was to the nanny, how he relaxed into her arms, in a way he did not with her, how he looked at Clara with a loving shine to his eyes. Felix clung to Clara, and Violet felt only gratitude, relief that her previous behaviour had not affected him too badly and that Clara was now compensating for his mother's inadequacies, which might otherwise have caused him harm.

'You are being collected for the asylum.'

Donna looked happy.

'Who is collecting me? I have no family.' Why was she feeling so confused? Since the electric shock treatment she had felt light headed and irresponsible. The visions had vanished to be replaced by a colourful, amenable world.

Why had she not recognised this before? How free she was?

'He says he is your uncle.'

'All my uncles are dead.'

'Do you want to be released or not?' The doctor looked angry.

Is he something to do with this, she wondered? She quickly thought, I have to get out, if this is the only way to escape, I should go along with it.

A carriage was waiting at the door. It was a brand new hansom cab. This was strange. And how odd to be in her old tatty clothes again. They smelt musty and unclean but this was the beginning of her new life.

'Good bye, Donna,' the doctor said. 'It has been a pleasure to have you with us.'

As soon as she clambered up into the empty cab, it started to drive away, the horses galloping faster and faster. The carriage rocked from side to side but heading in the opposite direction to London. Where am I going, she wondered, but she was past caring. Soon she would be able to dance again, put on her red shoes. How she loved to dance. The leaves of the trees shimmered in the darkness and the wind blew past her as they drove. The trees became thicker and thicker. Finally the horses came to a halt in the middle of a forest.

A man came out to greet her. He was wearing a long cloak and a hat that shielded the face.

'I'm so glad to meet you, Donna.'

'How do you know my name?'

He shrugged his shoulders.

'Thank you for getting me out of the asylum. I thought I would die in there.'

'No,' he said. 'I would not let you die in there.'

He took her hand. She felt so unbearably happy to be free of the asylum. She hardly knew what she was doing. She felt

*she was in a dream or a strange fairy tale, and this was her
prince come to rescue her. She had been waiting for this all
her life. He took her to a tunnel in the hill and they entered it,
a cavernous tunnel in the hill. The darkness seemed to caress
her skin and his strong hand holding her arm, leading the
way, seemed to comfort her.*

*She began to wonder if she were still in the asylum and
this was a mad dream. They entered a room fashioned from
the rock. It was like a cave with a table and bookcase. The
bookshelf was empty.*

*She began to feel uneasy. But the treatment had left her
with a wonderful feeling that she was untouchable.*

'Sit on the bed, Donna.'

*She watched as he started to prepare something. He was
getting out a hook, which he was attaching to a metal bar in
the ceiling.*

'Would you like a drink of water?' he asked.

She nodded.

*He brought over a jug from the table and poured out some
water for her. She drank it obediently. Obeying the commands
of others was what she had been doing for years in the asylum
and she was so grateful to be out in the real world. She was
beginning to feel drowsy, as if drugged by the same medicine
they had used to sedate her in the asylum, when she became
too difficult.*

'Do you like fairy tales?'

She nodded.

He brought out a fairy tale book.

'Would you like to rifle through and select one?'

She did as he asked; there were so many.

She came to 'The Red Shoes'. 'This one,' she said.

'Ah, you like to dance. You have such pretty feet.'

She looked down at her feet encased in their old black

patent boots. How could he tell, she wondered, that she did indeed have pretty feet.

After she lost consciousness and collapsed onto the floor, he carefully untied the laces of her boots. Her feet were small and delicate. He undressed her completely. She had red pubic hair to match both her hair and also the story, he thought approvingly. It was all meant to be. And she had beautiful full milky white breasts. He wondered how long it had been since a man had touched her and he stroked her breasts gently but the nipples remained inert. He stroked down the inner side of her soft thighs.

He made a square incision on her back, began delicately to peel back the skin. It was exquisite white skin, he thought, and he was careful not to tear it. It was so soft. He brought the knife up, still dripping with blood, and pressed it against her face.

Chapter 19

Violet bounced Felix up and down on her knees. He giggled with pleasure, his round cheeks like a doll's, she thought, an impossibly perfect porcelain doll. Archie was lying on the lawn, a few feet away, reading a newspaper. Felix was laughing and Violet was laughing because he was laughing. He was getting wrapped up in her long dress as they lay on the grass. The sun was beating down and butterflies were skimming the foxgloves and peonies, turquoise wings and pink and white petals a confusion of colour. For a brief moment she wondered if it was all a dream and she was still in the asylum.

She traced Felix's cheek with her finger. How warm his skin was, the opposite of the cold harsh texture of the asylum. He was life, as the asylum had been death. She buried her face in the nape of his neck, smelt his warm sugary scent, burning hot with life and needs, a flame of energy. He was hers. She had given birth to this wondrous creature. It was a miracle she still couldn't quite believe in, this act of creation. Before the asylum she had felt her life was constructed by thought, would fall apart without it, but now she could see that the opposite was true, life would happen quite happily without any thinking at all; she didn't need to worry or ponder or deliberate or imagine anything at all.

But then she looked up to see Archie staring at her strangely.

'Why were you looking at me like that?' she asked. He looked surprised. She hardly ever saw him surprised. It was as if everything that happened to him had already been expected by him.

'Was I, darling? I didn't mean to. Probably just admiring the perfection of the scene.'

'No,' she said. 'You weren't staring like that, it was more as if you didn't recognise who I was, that I was a strange object you were hoping to add to your collection.'

He laughed. 'I collect books. Not people. But if I did collect people I would certainly collect you.'

He was pandering to her but she felt reassured. She needed to know she was special to him. Felix clambered off her and started to crawl across the garden, just as Clara was coming up the path, carrying a basket of fruit she had picked from the greenhouses. Violet glanced at Archie to see if he had seen Clara approach in her white muslin dress and a large-brimmed straw hat, her golden hair overshadowing her face so Violet couldn't see her expression, just the shape of her voluptuous body, but Archie was looking at Felix.

Clara bent down to take Felix. Archie returned to reading his newspaper. Violet thought it odd that Archie did not acknowledge Clara. It was as if he were deliberately ignoring her. It was out of character, as he had the manners of a gentleman. Clara didn't seem to notice.

'Can you give Felix his tea?' Violet asked her. 'Archie and I want to stay out in the sun a little longer.'

'Of course, Lady Murray,' the nanny said. 'He *is* in the sun.'

And Violet felt a mild rebuke in her conversational tone, then thought, it's just my imagination and he has his hat on, anyway.

Later, in the kitchen, she asked, 'Clara, do you not miss having anyone in your life?'

'I need a husband like yours!'

'Well, he doesn't have to be exactly like Archie,' Violet replied with a laugh. And a pain struck her heart at the thought she could have married anyone else.

'I don't like men,' Clara said quickly.

'What do you mean?'

'They do repulsive things.'

Violet was astonished. Clara hadn't seemed puritanical.

'You mean making love?'

But Clara blushed furiously at the phrase. Violet laughed.

'I know it seems repulsive but it's not when you're actually doing it. It's strange, it becomes more than it is.'

'It's what animals do.'

'True.'

'But we're not animals. We are made in the image of our Creator.'

'Yes, of course,' Violet said, hastily. 'So, you've never had a suitor? Even a kiss?'

Clara shook her head vehemently. 'A man's lips on mine.' She pursed her beautiful lips in a moue of disgust. 'It makes me shudder.'

CHAPTER 20

THE FOLLOWING WEEK there was a knock on the front door. The housemaid was busy polishing the silver, so Violet went to answer it. An hunched old man, stinking of drink, was standing there, looking at her lewdly. His eyes were bloodshot and his brown suit covered in patches. She noticed he had a convict's number tattooed on his neck. She wanted to shut the door immediately but he had wedged his foot in the doorframe.

'What do you want?'

'I've come to see Clara.'

'Clara!' She was astonished. She couldn't put her fragrant Clara and this man together.

'Why do you want to see Clara?'

'Important business.' He fell towards her and she quickly stepped out of his way and now he was standing inside the hall entrance. He was a big man; she couldn't force him out.

'Come into the kitchen.'

She led him to the kitchen where he sprawled on a chair. Seeing the astonished look on the cook's round homely face, Violet dismissed her.

'Clara has done very well for herself,' he said.

'She's a wonderful nanny.'

A look of panic crossed his deeply lined, hard features.

'A nanny?'

'Yes. You seem surprised.'

'No, No. Clara with children, that's all.'

'What do you mean?'

'Nothing, nothing. Didn't think she got on with children, that's all.'

She was puzzled. Archie had told her she had helped bring up her two younger brothers.

'She gets on fine with Felix. He adores her.'

Again that look of anxiety. Why was he looking so worried?

Just at that moment Clara came into the kitchen. As she saw the man sitting there, a look of utter horror crossed her face, quickly replaced by a forced smile of welcome.

'Father!' she said.

'Dearest,' he said as he got up and staggered towards her to embrace her.

She could see Clara trying not to take a step back.

'They've let you out.'

'Indeed. Finally.'

'That's wonderful,' Violet said, though she could see in Clara's eyes it was not.

'So where are you staying?'

'Down in the village. The inn. I'm looking for work.'

Clara looked at Violet quickly and then looked away.

'What kind of work?'

'Any. Gardening, hard labour.'

Violet felt speechless. Was she supposed to say something? Offer this uncouth man some kind of employment?

He suddenly looked very pale. 'May I lie down? I'm feeling tired.'

His eyelids were drooping and his movements languid. He was moving more slowly and clumsily than ever.

'Of course.'

'I'll take him to my room,' Clara said.

'Use one of the spare bedrooms. It will be fine.'

'Thank you, madam.'

She heard his faltering footsteps on the staircase and then Clara returning.

She looked sheepish.

'I'm so sorry, Lady Murray. Someone must have told him where I was working.'

'That's all right.'

Clara was looking down at the floor. Violet knew what she was feeling and thinking, as she often had that feeling of being over-responsible.

'Would you like me to find him some work, Clara? I could ask Bea if she needs anyone. She is very fond of you and I'm sure would like to help.'

'That would be wonderful.'

Her face lit up.

'I know all about madness,' Clara added.

'What do you mean?'

'It runs in my family. My father.'

This explained Clara's self-contained nature, Violet thought. It was not about emotional placidity but about secrecy. She was very private. She now knew why Clara worked so assiduously. She wondered what form her father's madness took.

That night at dinner she discussed the subject with Archie. She told him that Bea had agreed to take on Clara's father to help her in the garden, that she didn't mind his background.

'So, Clara's father. A drunkard and convict. There's a surprise. And her so prim and proper.'

He seemed amused.

'And you're not worried about him harming Felix?'

'No. He will do him no harm. If he's Clara's father, he'll be too scared. He'll probably keep away.'

'What on earth do you mean? Clara isn't scary.'

Archie looked non-plussed. 'Scared is the wrong word. I meant he won't want to let her down. She sets such high standards.'

'Oh yes, I see what you mean.'

She toyed with her duck breast. She felt it slightly odd the way he talked about Clara, as if he knew her in ways she didn't.

'You do like Clara, don't you?' Archie asked. 'You don't think her too reserved? Not enough fun for Felix? After what happened he needs fun.'

'Of course I like her. And she's good for him.'

'He needs security. Even more than fun,' Archie continued. 'And that is what Clara gives him. Put her father to work in Bea's garden. Then everyone will be happy.'

A few days later, Violet was in the drawing room when she heard persistent crying coming from the nursery. Thinking Clara must be outside, she went upstairs but to her surprise, Clara was already in the nursery, standing by the cot. Her arms were outstretched as if about to pick up Felix, who had his arms lifted up towards her. But Clara, with an odd smile on her face, then slowly let her arms fall to her side. Felix's crying intensified. He didn't understand what was happening.

'Clara, what on earth are you doing? You're upsetting him. He thinks you are going to pick him up!'

Clara turned around, surprised, not having seen Violet come in.

'It's just a game.'

'Well, it's a cruel game. Please don't play it any more.'

Clara immediately reached down into the cot and Felix tottered into her arms, ecstatic. That behaviour, Violet thought, will make him more dependent on her. If he thinks he may lose her, he will crave her comfort all the more. Is that why she was doing it? Or was it, as she said, just a silly game? She thought of Archie, his absences, and how dependent on him she had grown. Do people learn to manipulate the emotions of others instinctively, she wondered?

'Can I have him, Clara?' she asked.

But Felix started to cry again when Clara tried to give him over to Violet. He clung to Clara fiercely as if frightened to let go.

'Keep him, Clara.'

Was there that odd smile again, about Clara's lips, or had she just imagined it? Perhaps it was just delight that Felix loved her so much. But that game Clara had been playing with Felix – she didn't like it.

That evening she mentioned what had happened to Archie, expecting him to understand her concern. But instead he looked cross.

'Clara is doing a very good job. In fact you would be lost without her.'

'I know. I'm grateful. But I thought it a strange game. Even cruel.'

'I don't think you are in the right position to judge.'

She took a sharp intake of breath.

'I was ill. That's unfair.'

He was so good at echoing her own critical thoughts, confirming what she already thought about herself.

'Yes, I am sorry,' he said, with a smile, and came over and put his arms around her. 'Don't worry. Clara would not have meant to be cruel. She would just have been playing with him. She's been a Godsend to us. Please don't do anything to lose her. Look how Felix loves her.'

And she could see Felix how loved Clara. He would crawl

over to her, and Clara would take him in her arms and lift him up and swing him round as he giggled.

She didn't really want to think any more about what she had seen – she wanted to consider Clara as pure as she looked, like an angel from heaven. She wanted to block out any vision of Clara other than the one she needed her to be. Her own version of herself had become unstable and various.

From the drawing room window, the next day, she observed Clara in the garden with Felix. It was a halcyon picture, Clara sitting on the lawn, her hair shining in the sunlight as Felix crawled around her in circles, laughing infectiously, his smile lighting up his ecstatic face. Violet saw Archie strolling across the garden towards them. She watched as he bent down and picked up Felix, cradling him in his arms. He exchanged a few words with Clara, who looked bashfully down, as he addressed her. They made a handsome couple, Violet thought, the two of them together: one charismatic, the other passive.

That night she dreamt she was following Archie down a tunnel. It was a dark labyrinth carved into a cliff face. Tunnels were veering off in all directions but she could follow his imprints in the dusty rocky ground, as if they were bread-crumbs. She heard vague screams from the end of the tunnel, a woman's screams. Her heart was beating faster. She turned round and ran back out through the tunnel into the sunlight.

Chapter 21

ARCHIE HAD BEEN away on a business trip for days and Violet had woken up during a hot summer's night, warm and restless, her long white cotton nightgown clinging to her skin. Compelled, as if she were sleepwalking, pulled along by a power external to herself, she went downstairs to the drawing room where the piano stood by the window. She opened the lid and put her hands on the keys. The ivory was cool and hard to her touch, reassuringly solid compared to the unreality of her feelings and surroundings. The moon was shining through the window, reflecting off the polished wood of the piano as if it were made of glass.

She had not played music since giving birth to Felix. It seemed too risky, as if somehow she would be giving something up of herself that she could not afford to spare. She tried a few notes, but it was as if she had forgotten how to play. She stood up and closed the lid.

'Why don't you play a tune, madam?'

Startled, she turned around. Clara was standing in the doorway. How long had she been standing there, watching her?

'I don't feel like it, Clara.'

'Lord Murray told me you play well.'

An uneasy discovery that they talked to each other behind her back, even if it was to compliment her on her piano playing. She was being paranoid again. She should be flattered. It was since she had returned from the asylum that she had become worried that people were talking about her behind her back.

'Oh,' she said.

'He was just being nice,' Clara said and quietly left the room.

Violet sat down at the piano again and opened the lid. As if her hands were possessed, she started to play the piano with a passion and intensity new to her. It was only after she had started playing that she realised it was Schumann, his visionary intensity flowing through her fingers.

She felt unable to stop. Sweat began to pour down her face and she was growing tired. Only after an hour did her fingers finally stop moving and she lifted her hands from the keyboard. She leant her cheek on the surface of the piano, the wood cool against her hot skin.

Betsy had been let out of the asylum a few weeks before and was walking down the village high street, late at night. She had been sewing all day at her mother's house and was exhausted. She couldn't wait to get back to her little house. Her husband would be out as usual, drinking in the local pub. She had brought back the shirt that had been ordered. The customer was coming round that night. Soon after she returned home, there was a knock on the door. A figure stood in the doorway, in the shadows so she couldn't see his face.

'Have you my shirt?'

'I do.'

He spoke with a posh accent. Betsy felt impressed. She wanted to impress him.

'I need to check it will fit. Would you mind accompanying me to my home? Put on your cloak.'

They walked down the dark streets of the village and up a long driveway. She could see no lights.

'It's a long walk,' she murmured.

'Indeed it is.' And she felt the knife go into her side, between the ribs, long and hot pain. Her heavy cloak soaked up the blood and he lay her down gently in the driveway in the darkness.

'What do you want from me?' she asked.

'What is skin deep,' he replied.

'I don't understand.'

'What I mean is I want nothing from you at all.'

He watched her die under the branches of the tree. Her head fell back to catch the moonlight so he could see her face more clearly. Her dark complexion paled as the lifeblood seeped from her. He lifted her up over his shoulder, easily. She was light and ill fed.

He walked through the forest until he reached the tunnel that led into the underground rooms. It had once been a rich man's folly. He lit the candles. It was so still down there. No wind stirred. He lay her down on the ground and pulled the knife from her side. Without it, she looked just as though she were sleeping.

Should he take the skin off first? He took off her heavy woollen cloak, which left heavy bloodstains on his hands. She was wearing a corset beneath her grey linen dress. He laid out her arms so they were outstretched. He then brought the blade of his knife down beneath the arm socket.

He then hung her up on the hook and finally began to peel off her skin. It was all so elaborate, he thought, as he left the skin to dry. He had to be patient. The process took days.

That afternoon, Clara rushed into the kitchen, where Violet was telling the cook what to prepare for supper. Clara's face was flushed with excitement. She was carrying a book concealed under her arm. She stopped, startled to see Violet in the kitchen, as if she had been waiting for her. The cook, sensing a strained atmosphere, left to gather herbs from the garden.

'What on earth have you got there?' Violet asked. She could see the gilt edge of the pages.

She was puzzled. Sometimes she forgot Clara had a life apart from her life helping her. It was a shock she might have plans and secrets of her own. What was Clara really like under her quiet placid manner, playing with Felix, cutting up his fruit into the shape of hearts with her small knowing hands? Clara looked up with her wide eyes.

'Oh,' she said, 'just a book. Archie has asked me to fetch him a book.'

Violet noticed pinpricks on her neck like red dots of infectious marks.

'Have you hurt your neck?'

Clara put her hand to her neck.

'Oh no. I noticed those, too. Insect bites, I suppose.'

She gave her that sweet smile. Violet tried to look beyond the sweetness, to read duplicity into it, but could not. She was just going to ask her again about the book but Felix came in and the moment passed as Clara quickly took Felix into the garden to play ball.

A forest of heavy oaks surrounded the garden of the house. Violet rarely went in to it. The trees grew too close together and blocked out the light. They murmured when the wind blew through their leaves. At winter they looked bare, like skeletons. In summer they looked dense and impenetrable as if hiding secrets. Sometimes she wondered if the forest was like her marriage. Full of secrets, obscure, and underneath as hard and unforgiving as bone.

She went back to her husband's study. She took down the painting and unlocked the safe door. It was empty. The book had gone. Her utter devastation and anger were beyond all reason. She was seized by panic.

She found Clara in the laundry room.

'Give me the book.'

'What do you mean?'

'That book you were carrying under your arm the other day. It was the fairy tale book, wasn't it? You have stolen it from the safe.'

'You have become delusional, madam. Lord Murray has told me how that book preoccupies you.'

What was he doing, discussing this with Clara? 'He is the one obsessed by it. He keeps it in a safe, for God's sake. And now it's gone.'

'I'm sorry, I don't know anything about that.'

Violet looked into Clara's placid, apparently willing face and found no response in those grey eyes, no flicker of defensiveness or excitement.

Violet tried to become accustomed to the fact that the book had gone, accept its loss as just another event, but could not. She went around as if part of her heart had been removed.

The following afternoon Clara came into the drawing room. Violet noticed that Clara was muddy.

'Clara, what have you been doing? You are covered in mud.'

Clara looked startled.

'Oh, playing with Felix in the woods.'

Clara looked at Felix in her arms. His baby clothes were spotless and his hands were clean.

'Why isn't Felix muddy then?'

Clara gave her a slow smile. 'Oh, I carried him on my back. I didn't want him to get muddy, too.'

'That was very nice of you, Clara.'

Felix looked up and smiled at Clara.

'Did Clara give you a nice piggyback ride in the forest?'

But before Felix could smile in reply, Clara quickly said, 'Time for tea, Felix,' and whisked him away.

Chapter 22

VIOLET KNEW VERY little about her husband. She never talked about her own late parents and never asked about his either. It had been enough for her that he suggested by his manner, his culture, his cultivation, that he had a history – had a life of elite university education, sophisticated women and select friendships.

She went to the bookshelf in the library that contained miscellany. She found a single photograph album in dark crimson leather tucked away on a bottom shelf. She took the album outside into the garden and, sitting on a bench, opened it up at random. There, towards the end of the album, was a photograph of their registry wedding, Archie, her, the witnesses and the minister. And then a photograph of her in their marriage bed, holding the newborn Felix in her arms. Flicking backwards, she found an older photograph of Archie as a young boy. He was standing in front of their house, his parents standing on either side of him, but how alone he seemed, as if he was deliberately keeping himself apart from them.

She opened the book at random on another page. There was a photograph of a woman, looking as if she were asleep, in the same marriage bed, another newborn baby apparently asleep in her arms. Violet studied her still face. Yes, the bookshop man had been right, she could see a physical similarity to herself in this death picture of Rose and her child.

A dragonfly hovered about the lawn with its buzzing sound. She hated the way they flew – like machines. Then silence. She looked up. It had landed near her on a wooden chair. How ugly it looked with its thin linear body like an exclamation mark and its black and yellow pattern.

There was a final photo. A recent one of Archie, she judged, by his imperceptibly aged appearance. Standing next to him was a slightly older voluptuous woman in an over-furnished opulent drawing room. She looked dark and sensual as if a slave to predictable appetites. She wore a heavily brocaded golden and blue dress with a wide sash tied at her unnaturally narrow waist.

Archie looked different in this photograph, more uncertain and secretive. His face seemed the product of a different kind of situation, standing so near to the older woman. But the look in his eyes was the same, detachedly amused at a private joke. She felt convinced this woman had some kind of power over him. She turned the photograph over. On the back Archie had just scribbled *Lavinia*.

What was the private joke, she wondered? She stood up slowly – she would take a walk to the edge of the estate to clear her mind. The sun was beating down on her, in spite of the large-brimmed hat she was wearing. It was so hot, unnaturally hot. The long grasses around her stroked her bare legs. It was even too warm for the birds, except for the occasional brave chirrup. It was nearing noon. It was as if her idyll had been petrified in the heat. Had become a nightmare version of its former self, all still hard lines of a surrealist painting. Even the small fluttering of the tiny black butterflies suddenly looked like batwings.

The heat was making her jump from one hallucinatory image to the next. It was then she saw her, lying outstretched on the field near the edge of a stream, a woman concealed in the long grass. The shadows of the leaves of the trees above were playing delicately on her face. As Violet drew nearer she could see the woman was posed in a shape of a star. Her right arm was missing. It had been cut off below the socket. Blood had soaked the grass around her, as if she had bled to death, and was running into the stream. Iron rings had tethered her to the ground. Blood had also run in intricate rivulets, following the lines of the feathers of a large swan's wing. The wing had been placed on the ground in place of the missing arm. It looked as if the swan's wing was sprouting naturally from the empty arm socket.

The woman's body had been eviscerated, turned inside out. The entrails were spilling out like so many question marks. Violet resisted the convulsions in her throat, the desire to retch.

The body had been skinned carefully, all skin removed. It did not look like a human being now, but that is how we all look, she thought, under the skin, below the illusion of our surface. The head remained intact. The pretty face of Betsy looked up, her eyes open, her mouth parted. Grey liquid oozed from the lips. Violet wondered if it were semen.

She couldn't believe she was observing this scene with such a sense of detachment, and somewhere in the back of her mind she wondered if she were in shock. Who or what had done this to Betsy? Was it a man, or animal? Or someone who was both?

She looked up. She thought she saw a dark shadow move behind the trees. She wanted to scream but couldn't. She turned and ran through the fields back into the cool hallway of the house. She felt unable to think clearly. She had to think clearly. Through the hall window she could see Clara with Felix at the far end of the garden playing with a ball. How perfect the scene looked, the trees in full leaf. It was as if she could smell the roses and the herb garden with its strong, pungent scent of sage.

Perhaps what she had seen was just a return of the delusions. She had to compose herself. She looked at herself in the hall mirror, brushed down her hair and narrowed her widened panic-stricken eyes. She turned and walked slowly out into the garden. Should she approach them? But her appearance might unnerve them.

'Clara!' she cried out, but the word stuck in her throat. 'Clara,' she again shouted hoarsely, but it was no good, Clara couldn't hear her. She was too far away.

She walked over the gravel driveway onto the lawn. Her legs felt weak, her whole body was trembling. She had to appear calm. Felix must not see how distressed she was; it was important to protect him. The gravel was dry after so many rainless days. When she was halfway across the lawn, Felix saw her and started to wave. She waved back. Clara looked up and saw her.

Violet beckoned for her to come over to her. Clara threw the ball for Felix who crawled after it and Clara walked slowly towards her, a gentle smile on her face. She didn't realise how important this was, Violet thought, and she mustn't guess now, it must be kept hidden. Felix is a curious and sensitive child; if he sees anything strange it will upset him. As Clara approached, the sun caught her hair.

'What is it, Lady Murray?' If Clara had noticed anything strange about Violet, she didn't reveal it.

'Can you come with me, Clara?' she said. Clara turned to Felix and shouted out to him, clear as a bell, 'I'm just going into the house with mummy. I'll be back in a moment.'

Felix started throwing the ball straight up in the air.

The two women walked back to the house. As they reached the entrance, Violet said, 'Clara, I need to tell you something.

I've seen a body. A body of a woman from the asylum.'

Clara turned to her. Her expression had subtly altered, looked watchful rather than concerned.

'Lady Murray, you need to sit down. Have a rest. It's been hot.'

'I'm perfectly all right. I mean I'm not all right, I'm shocked. But by what I've seen. It's nothing to do with the heat.'

'Lady Murray, you looked flustered. We'll go into the kitchen. Have a cold drink. Lord Murray will be back soon.'

They were now in the hall. Violet felt like screaming at her.

'It's not a delusion. I saw it!'

'All right then. Where is it? I'll go and see.' Clara looked determined.

'No! No! You shouldn't. It's too shocking. I don't want you to see it. Wait for Archie.' Violet grasped her arm.

Clara took her firmly by the hand and led her into the empty kitchen. Violet sat down on a chair, feeling oddly cold. Clara poured her some water and Violet took the glass gratefully. Violet was gripping the glass so tightly that her fingers were drained of blood.

'Look, when you've calmed down, why don't you take me to it and show me. There will be nothing there. Nothing to fear.'

'No,' Violet whispered, hoarsely now. 'I can't see that again. What about the blood?'

'There will be no blood.'

'How on earth do you know that? I *saw* the blood.' Then suddenly she was filled with self-doubt. 'Don't tell my husband about this, Clara? Promise.'

She didn't want to be put back in the asylum.

'Of course not, Lady Murray. I understand. It is just one of your turns.'

'Because of the heat.'

'Because of the heat. Are you all right now? Because I'd better get back to Felix, he'll be waiting for me.

'Of course, Clara. Thank you so much for being so understanding.'

'Not at all, Lady Murray.'

Violet sipped the rest of her drink. It had been a delusion. A mild delusion. Because of the heat.

Violet saw through the window Clara walking across the lawn, back to Felix who had been playing happily on his own with his ball.

CHAPTER 23

THAT EVENING CLARA gave Violet a strong sedative to help her sleep. Violet woke up in bed in the middle of the night with a throbbing headache. She turned over to see if Archie was lying beside her. The bed was empty. There was just space where he should have been. Her head felt so sore, it was as if someone had struck her there. She didn't even remember going to bed. Someone, presumably Clara, must have undressed her, put her nightgown on, and laid her in the bed. But how had she got upstairs? Had she been semi-conscious? She couldn't remember. Clara was not strong enough to have carried her up by herself.

She looked at her arms for bruises or marks where she might have been accidentally hurt but there were none. She carefully slid out of bed, taking care not to make any sudden movement in case it exacerbated the throbbing in her head. She needed more medication now to ease the pain. The curtains had not been drawn and the moon was shining strangely brightly through the window, giving out an uncanny light. Where was he, she wondered? She padded down the corridor, to the stairs. The soft carpet comforted her as she was feeling increasingly strange and incoherent.

She heard murmuring from the kitchen. She opened the door.

Sitting opposite each other at the kitchen table were Archie and Clara, both fully dressed. They appeared to be in deep conversation.

They looked up, startled, as they heard her come in.

'Violet! What are you doing here, my love?' Archie asked.

Putting her on the defensive, she thought.

'I'm looking for a pill for a headache. What are you doing down here with Clara?'

'Oh, discussing Felix.'

She felt furious at Archie for his patronising manner, as if she was somehow intruding on an important discussion between him and Clara. As if she were the employee, instead of Clara.

Clara was looking at Violet with a mild, pleasant expression. As if this all had hardly anything to do with her at all. As if she were a dandelion seed blown here on the wind into her kitchen, Violet thought. She felt oddly proprietorial. She felt like an animal. Why? She felt like a cornered animal.

'Get out of my kitchen, Clara. Now. Get out.'

'I'm sorry, madam. We really were just trying to help.'

She left abruptly.

Archie was looking at Violet with an expression of astonishment and rage.

'What the hell do you think you are doing, Violet? Being so rude to Clara. She was just trying to help.'

Violet felt so angry, tears were pricking her eyes.

'Why are you taking her side? What about me?'

'You're sounding like a jealous wife.'

Violet turned, unable to speak.

'And why can't you discuss things with me?' she hissed.

'Because we didn't want to worry you. Clara told me about your seeing a body. She has been worried about you.'

Horror struck her heart. Her head was pounding. She was beginning to shake. She had confided in Clara, and Clara had betrayed her trust.

'So that's what you were discussing with Clara! You think I'm losing my mind again!'

'Don't be silly, Violet. We know you're fully recovered. The asylum has cured you. You would never harm Felix again.'

Why did she feel Archie was threatening her rather than reassuring her? That moon was still shining into the kitchen, covering everything in its silvery sheen, making everything look out of a fairy tale. But what fairy tale, she thought, trying to grasp for the answer. I've got to work out which fairy tale it is. She lost consciousness and slid to the floor, blackness engulfing her.

CHAPTER 24

O VER THE NEXT few days, as the weather cooled, Violet realised how foolish she was being. Archie and Clara were just trying to protect her. Was what had happened connected to her own inner darkness? The skies were no longer a hectic blue but a peaceful balmy grey. It grew thunderous, with a noticeable pressure in the air, but she still felt better than in the arid heat with the sun burning down, turning the grass to the colour of beaten yellow straw.

One afternoon in the village she saw Clara walking down the street. Archie was walking by her side. Her pale skin and rosy lips were like a young child's, Violet thought. She became overtaken by Clara's lustrous and sensual anima. As if who Violet was, her own sense of sensuality, was disappearing. The incarnation of Clara, all flesh, was reducing Violet to an ethereal spirit. Ah, the twists and turns of relationships, the inconsistencies, the realisation that nothing was certain, no one wholly dependable. But Archie was. Archie gave her that certainty that she could trust him. Violet had only just managed to collect herself, when Clara and Archie disappeared from sight.

The next morning, as Felix played with a jigsaw of a few large wooden pieces on the drawing room floor, Violet knelt down beside him. She looked at Felix, enjoying the shape of his head, the outline of him. It was so peaceful, that absolute love for him. Different from the romantic feelings she had for men, which were edgy and electric. This love for her child consumed her for that moment. It was hardly to do with him or her. It seemed to exist apart from them both. She would never forget this feeling, she thought, as she watched him play.

She turned her attention to the jigsaw. It was a jigsaw she had never seen before and she wondered if Archie or Clara had bought it for him. It depicted three scenes from fairy stories. One scene showed Elise throwing her eleven nettle shirts over her eleven brothers in 'The Wild Swans', to transform the princes from swans back into men. Violet could clearly see the youngest brother still brandishing one wing for an arm. The scene from 'The Little Mermaid' showed the mermaid, having had her tail transformed into legs by the witch, dancing with the prince, but feeling as if she were walking on the sharp edge of swords. Violet could see the blood flowing from the mermaid's legs. The third scene was from 'The Red Shoes'. Here the headsman was cutting off the dancer's feet imprisoned in the red shoes, so that she could finally stop her relentless dancing. Violet quickly cleared the floor of the jigsaw as Felix started to cry.

'It's not right for you,' she said and swept him up in her arms.

Just then, Clara came into the drawing room. 'There is a visitor for you,' Clara announced and firmly took the crying Felix from Violet's arms and left the room. A moment later, a man walked in, strangely, a bit like a marionette, as if his legs were slightly out of control. It was oddly endearing.

'Good morning. Lady Murray?'

She looked at him. He was tall and thin. Rarefied. Unsmiling. He seemed so spiky, like a skeleton was popping out of his skin, long, thin limbs, knobbly joints. Even his hands looked long and thin, like a sketcher's lines, delineated rather than fleshed out. His eyes were high up in his face, like an Egyptian god, but it was his intelligence that radiated out, quietly and insistently. He was probably younger than he looked, but marked out by what he had seen.

'I'm Detective Benedict. I wonder if you would mind answering some questions?'

She could tell by his overly polite manner that he probably thought little of her. She was just another privileged, kept woman on a country estate with a self-entitled husband. Loneliness was the price she paid for all this luxury and beauty. She was the absolute sum of her parts. She could see it all in his insolent blue eyes.

She nodded. 'Of course.'

'I'm afraid I have to inform you that women have been disappearing from the nearby asylum.'

She felt sick, disheartened. She nodded. She couldn't mention her hallucination of Betsy's body in the field. They would put her back in the asylum. Take Felix away from her.

'You haven't seen anything suspicious in the area. Heard anything in the village?' A sudden thought struck her. Had someone sent the detective to her, to trick her into mentioning her delusion?

'I don't really go out much.'

Adrenaline was pouring though her.

'And what time does your husband usually come home?'

'About nine.'

'That's quite late.' He sat down in Archie's chair.

'He works very hard.'

She didn't tell him about the nights he disappeared.

Why wasn't he writing anything down, she wondered? He was one of those people with a good memory. He didn't have to do anything but sit there and watch her. She felt almost overcome by his intelligence as if it was part of his sexuality. But she knew she had an intelligence to match his. She often noticed it was only when we shared the same qualities that we recognised them in other people. Kind people recognised kindness in others. Unkind people saw kindness as a weakness to be exploited. Violet had always been slow to recognise malice.

'Children?'

'We have one son, Felix.'

He had a quality of listening absolutely to her as if he was taking in every word she said. She had to be careful. She thought. What was wrong with her, this odd susceptibility to an utter stranger? He was just presenting a version of himself, just doing his job.

'Servants?'

'Yes, and our nanny, Clara. But she is like one of the family.'

She felt oddly displaced now; the stress had depleted her. If only she could find the book. She knew it would have all the answers, this book of fairy tales. But there was a look in his eyes, drawing her in. She should know better by now, she thought, not to be drawn in by someone's perceptiveness. It was her undoing.

'But one of our books has gone missing from the safe.' She was taking a risk saying this, of unintended consequences, but she wanted him to find it.

'A book?'

'A book of fairy tales.'

'Ah. Valuable?'

'Very. First edition.'

He was still lounging in Archie's armchair. His long legs dangled like a grasshopper's. His face was impassive, except for those eyes. They were still staring at her.

'Would you like me to do a quick search of her room?' asked the detective.

She felt her face flushing.

She looked out of the window to see Clara wheeling the pram outside.

'That would be very kind of you.'

She gave him directions to Clara's room, but he came back a few minutes later with his hands empty.

'Can you think of any reason the book may have gone missing?'

His tweed suit looked soft, she thought. Cuddly clothes, she thought, for someone not very cuddly.

'Just that the book is valuable.'

'Well, we'll check the bookshops. See if it's been handed over as stolen goods. We'll ask around the village.'

'Thank you.'

She suddenly thought, he's not interested in this at all. He doesn't care. And why should he – when women are going missing? She shook herself, as if trying to shake off this image of what she had become, a ghost, a woman covered in cobwebs, a woman who no longer inhabited her own life but trespassed over it.

That evening, having dinner with Archie, she looked at his face for clues. She knew that if she asked about the missing book he would tell her more of his white lies. She would have lost whatever advantages she had, the power of her secret knowledge. As long as she had this power he wouldn't be able to bamboozle her with the plausibility of his deception. He looked the same. And again she wondered, is this an act? Is this all an act? *How real are you, Archie?*

CHAPTER 25

S HE NEEDED TO find out about the provenance of the
book. She decided to go back to the bookshop. She dressed
in a simple grey dress but she put up her hair, and painted her
lips deep plum. She did this without thinking but her heart
was beating faster. She did not like to think why she wanted
to make an impression on him. Taking that first step along
the path to betrayal, that inevitable, tiny innocent step, which
contained the seed of corruption within it.

She entered the shop, and the opening door set off the
ringing of the bell. The young man was standing by one of the
shelves. He was putting a book back on the shelf and looked
round at her when he heard the bell. When he saw her he
didn't smile, but finished putting the book back on the shelf
and came towards her.

'Can I help?'

'I wonder if you might have been sold a book of fairy tales,
recently. A first edition?'

He shook his head but after a slight hesitation. Was he
lying? He looked at her laconically.

He was beautiful, she thought, more beautiful than her,
with his golden hair, his face flushed, like a lion, she thought.
Be brave, she said to herself, be brave. But as she looked at him
she realised that it wasn't just up to her. He had to be brave,
too. And that didn't seem to be possible. And perhaps that

was for the best. Safer. To stay on either side of the chasm. Not looking down and not trying to cross, the wind blowing in their hair. She touched one of the books. She touched the leather.

His dark eyes, almost black, were full of fear and she wondered if her own dark ones were too. What were they scared of? Of desire leaving a shell of good intentions behind itself. Why take that risk? It would be mad. This desire for a future to be different from the one taken by default. She wanted him to embrace her, to take charge, have the courage of his conviction. But he didn't, he remained hesitant and they were left standing on either side of a chasm of possibility, staring at each other in disbelief.

She finally leaned forward and touched her lips with his. He stood there not responding but nor did he move back. She kissed him harder, her teeth clashing against his, and he brought his arms behind her and pulled her in close. Still kissing, they staggered into the narrow corridor and he brought her to the floor between the towering piles of books on either side.

'Do you remember me?' she whispered. 'Do you remember me?'

She lifted up her dress and climbed on top of him. His hands fumbled for her breasts beneath the folds of cloth. She was gasping with desire. She felt him hard between her legs before he entered her.

'I remember you,' he replied. She could see his face crease, as if in pain, before he came. He then buried his head in her chest, wanting to recover himself, not wanting to see her, or her to see him. He finally looked up at her, grateful. Men were so grateful, she thought, when it came to sex.

'I'm looking for the book of fairy tales,' she repeated. 'Have you seen it? It's dedicated to Rose.' The sex had loosened him, she could see. He thought she had given him something, so it was his turn now to return the favour.

They took a carriage into the centre of London. She felt more intimate with him in the little hansom, within its dark walls on hard seats, than she had when fucking him. She could see the lights flashing past, hear the sound of the hooves on the cobblestones. You could be truly intimate without speaking, she thought. There were no false promises, hurtful words. Histories could be rewritten and dreams realised.

It was an expensive restaurant in West London, a cavernous space with candlelight and modern décor of stained glass windows and wooden panelling. It seemed transparent, reflective and glittering. It was like being in a house made of glass, and it rendered Violet angelic and impatient. Walking into the restaurant, he didn't hold open the door for her. She felt this was deliberate in some way, a kind of resistance to being in her power, even if only within the deceptive rules of social etiquette. The head waiter then led them to a table in the centre of the room. They ordered from the menu. He had structural hands, she noticed, and those wide-apart black eyes, and that sneaky, mocking mouth.

After their first course was brought he started to eat. She waited a while before bringing out of her purse the photograph she had taken from the album of Lavinia and Archie together.

'Do you know who she is?'

He looked at the photograph she showed him. 'She is a bookbinder.'

Were they now bound together in their betrayal of Archie? Would he have to tell her everything?

'She binds rare books made of special leather. They are rare. There are collectors who value them more than anything. Books bound in a unique way.'

'They are bound for someone who has died?'

'Of course. A loved one, a lost daughter, son or uncle or husband. Lavinia is the most respected bookbinder in London. Her work is exquisite, each stitch done by her hand. These collectors are cultured people of huge intellect.'

'Do they have to be wealthy?'

'It certainly helps.'

'The fairy tale book is dedicated to Rose,' she repeated.

'She loved fairy tales.' There was a softness to his voice. Violet looked up, startled. The thought recurred to her that he had been infatuated by Rose. Were those tears in his eyes, or just the reflection of the candlelight? Had he found Violet attractive only because of her physical similarity to Rose? A terrible feeling of uncertainty welled up inside her about what was real and what was not.

He swiftly changed the subject. 'So what is Archie like as a husband?'

She didn't reply. She felt the need to protect Archie, that somehow he might fall into danger if she said anything about him at all.

'Violet?' He spoke so softly she only just heard him.

'Yes?'

'Just leave this alone. It won't be worth it. You have a good life. You love your husband. Forget about this stupid book. Forget about Lavinia. You won't learn anything new from her.' He spoke so insistently. Who is he protecting, she wondered? Was it himself? 'Don't rock the boat.'

'But look at the photo of Lavinia with him! She looks like she has some kind of hold over him.'

'You have too much imagination.'

She looked at him. She was aware that tendrils of her hair had fallen loose from where her hair had been tied up. She felt tired, but she now also felt sure.

'It's because I love him that I need to find out.'

'I will give you her address, if you want, but it will only be trouble. Heartache.'

'So it's better to remain happy and ignorant like a pig.'

'Isn't it obvious?'

'Not to me. I've never been scared of pain.'

But she was lying. She had married to avoid pain. She had lost herself in the arcadian countryside to avoid pain. Her whole married life had been a carefully constructed edifice to avoid pain. And it had worked well. Until she fell ill. She had once been content. Any dissatisfaction she had had with her marriage had been buried so deeply she had been hardly aware of it. Hadn't her life to all intents and purposes been perfect? She had been privileged and protected like a pig in a diamond-encrusted pigsty lined with red velvet cushions. She had never envisaged a different future. It had all been mapped out, unconsciously and inevitably.

And now she felt scared. Scared of what was happening. She would forget what had happened between her and the book assistant. It was nothing to do with her real life. She wanted to heal these cracks, these fissures that were spreading out over her life. Lacquer them over. Pretend they weren't happening. *The truth will set you free* came into her head and then she quickly supressed it. She didn't want to know the truth. She didn't need her freedom. She was happy as she was.

'We have to live with uncertainty,' he said. 'Your search for this book is an obsession because you can't live without knowing everything.'

He was right, she thought. This is the product of my illness. My hallucinations have led me down this road. But because of the delusions it is now so important for me to find out what is real.

She stood up. 'I'm so sorry, I've got to go.'

He remained sitting, nonchalant.

'I'm sorry you have to leave,' he said. 'But I understand.'

She staggered from the restaurant in a dream. She had to find somewhere quiet, be on her own, this was all so overwhelming. She discovered a small hotel in Bloomsbury and booked herself in, trying to ignore the porter's disapproving stares over how she was travelling alone.

CHAPTER 26

THE ADDRESS THE bookshop assistant had given her for Lavinia was in Belgravia. Violet took a carriage to the house. It was a large white stucco house in a grand square overlooking the gardens. She rang the bell.

A butler opened the shiny black door.

Violet stared at him, not quite knowing what to say.

'She is expecting you,' he said.

So, the man from the bookshop had let Lavinia know she was coming.

The butler led her up the wide staircase to the drawing room on the first floor. It was a large ornate room that overlooked the park with a heavy, intense, sweet smell that Violet couldn't quite place. The room was empty. She turned round to look for the butler but he had disappeared, having slipped out again quietly. She sat down in one of the plush velvet armchairs that enveloped her in its luxuriant softness. She tried to sit up straight.

The room was dense and opulent, full of heavy furnishings with deep purple colours and dark mahogany furniture. It was clearly demonstrative of a certain taste and sensibility. Someone of a very dominant personality, she thought, with wealth – whether inherited or not she didn't know. It was carefully constructed to look inherited, but she knew of people who bought the interiors of old country homes wholesale and recreated them in their London flats.

The thick dark red Persian carpet with its geometric design suggested a puzzle to the room that needed to be solved. The heavy book shelves were laden with leather bound books, carefully ordered. There was no dust anywhere, which gave the impression of the room being a stage set rather than actually lived in.

Stuffed animals stared at her from behind glass cases: weasels and wild cats with glassy eyes. A fox's hair was short and bristly, his nose pointed. He looked alert, but for the fact he was dead. A stuffed heron stood in the corner, its feathers dry and lustreless. On the table was a list of books – with various numbers next to each one. They were all on arcane subjects: astrology, fishing, taxidermy and human anatomy.

Violet began to feel uneasy in the room, unsettled by its mixture of carefully ordered ostentation and the neatly lined books, as if she were in a construct of someone's manipulative mind.

She could hear music being played in the distance, the resonant persistent sound of a harpsichord, the music running in on itself, a perpetual echoing of itself. She heard footsteps and the sound of the door being opened.

Violet took an instant dislike to the woman who was entering the room. She had straight dark hair that fell about an immobile face that would have been attractive with its small symmetrical features if it had not been for the staring, angry look in her eyes which made them as hard and glaring as those of her stuffed animals. She was draped in silks and smelled of incense, and Violet thought she would have made a plausible belly dancer or the wife of a wealthy baron. As Lavinia glided across the room, in her silk dress, her heavy gold and silver bangles jangled. Not only did she make her presence felt with her heavy pungent scent and billowy clothes that wafted around her but also with the clash of her jewellery as she moved her arms.

Violet watched from her chair, as Lavinia took out a book from a bookshelf and caressed its cover with her bejewelled fingers. The bangles clanged again. Her small but pouty mouth was pursed. Her scent wafted over Violet, invading her nostrils.

'They are beautiful objects, are they not?' She opened up a book at the flyleaf. Signed copies are the best. The inky residue of an author's genius.'

Violet looked around at the stuffed animals. They all seemed to be staring at her with the same watchful eyes as Lavinia. She noticed the name of the taxidermist on a small wooden panel engraved on each one: *Lavinia Dryden.*

Lavinia brought the book up to her nose and smelled it, flicked through the ancient thick ivory pages with faded print, the anatomy drawings of naked men and women. She weighed the book in her hand like a man weighing a woman's breast.

'Do you like books, Lady Murray?' Lavinia asked.

'Just to read,' Violet said.

'A mistake. A very big mistake. A poorly bound book disintegrates. Where would our learning be then? We need something permanent, solid. We need to treat words with the respect they are due. Treasure them. Adorn the books that contain these words with leather bindings, illuminate their words with gold. We shouldn't treat learning lightly.'

'But I would treat a word scrawled on a scrap of paper with the same respect as one written on an illuminated manuscript.'

'Then you are an unusual person. And very different from your husband.' Lavinia's mottled hands with thick fingers still held the book tightly. She handled the book expertly and again Violet was reminded of a lover manipulating a woman's body for his own pleasure. And then, as if breaking a spell, Lavinia quickly shut the book and put it on an occasional table, as if only then aware that she had been lost in reverie.

'So, what do you want?' Lavinia asked abruptly. It was more like a command.

'I hear you bind books.'

'Who did you hear that from?' She used questions as a method of attack.

'From a friend. I think he told you to expect me.'

Lavinia gave the most ugly smile Violet had ever seen, full of anger and insolence. Lavinia was still standing in the middle of the room, her personality so strong and furious that she seemed unaware of where either of them were.

'A book has gone missing from my husband's safe. A rare book.'

'And you think I stole it?'

'No. Of course not. But I wondered if someone might have given it to you to bind.'

Lavinia rang a bell. The butler entered. 'Bring me a sherry. Do you want something?'

Violet shook her head.

'One sherry. Dry. Sorry, what were you saying? Oh yes, a book your husband has lost.'

'Stolen. The book was stolen.'

'Yes, lost. What is the title?'

'It was a book of fairy tales.'

'Ah yes, his first wife liked fairy tales.'

'Except his first wife has died.'

'Indeed.' She picked up the anatomy book again from the table and gave it to Violet. 'Dead loved ones are used as memorabilia. And then sometimes not even dead ones.'

'What do you mean?'

The anatomy book had been freshly bound. She could see the skin of the cover, pale and fresh and soft to touch, like the fine fuzz of a rose. Violet dropped it back onto the table, her heart hurt and unsteady, her breath short.

'Don't become the object of affection. It's dangerous. Certain men want to possess you entirely. Men will do anything to satisfy their desires and this can lead men down paths they are powerless to resist.'

The loneliness of her marriage had led her inexorably to this woman, Violet thought. Lavinia was the witch who lived in the centre of the fairy tale forest. Violet was now in the witch's house where she might be given a spell to help her with her heart's desire, but at a certain price. Violet wondered if Lavinia had secretly desired Archie. You could never tell: people's attraction for certain types was utterly unpredictable. She still felt certain Lavinia exerted a secret power over Archie.

Violet stood up. 'Well, thank you for your time. I'm sorry to have bothered you.'

'I hope your husband finds his book.'

'Sentimental value, I think. Please let me know if you hear anything about it.'

'I will.'

As Violet was leaving the room, she heard Lavinia murmuring to the butler. 'Don't let her come in here again. She's over-susceptible. They are always the worst.'

Violet came out into the open air and took a deep breath, relieved to be free of Lavinia's profane and overpowering presence.

She felt she had been in the presence of an odd kind of madness, the kind of insanity generated by wealth, where people are spoilt and pampered and do not understand or tolerate what it is like not to get their way. A terrible overwhelming sense of privilege that they are completely unaware of. Where will has not been tempered by awareness of others. Violet had not come across this sense of entitlement before and it made her wonder to what lengths these kinds of people could go, what generic terrors or unhappiness could they unleash in the name of their desires?

Deep in thought, she stepped into the road just as the roar and clattering of a horse carriage clattered past. She leapt back just in time, the sound of rattling wheels and the beating of hooves resonating in her head. It was as if the carriage had come out of nowhere, like the horsemen of the apocalypse. It had seemed deliberate, as if the carriage had been trying to run her down.

She chided herself for being foolish and remembered Lavinia's comment about her being susceptible to her imaginings. This was just another case of her paranoia. Besides, who on earth would be wanting to kill her? She had no enemies. She had just been overwhelmed by Lavinia and her room and her animals and her books.

CHAPTER 27

S HE LOOKED OVER at her husband, sitting on the other side of the breakfast table in the morning light. She felt guiltless about her infidelity. It was as if it had never happened. She needed him, she depended on him for everything, her livelihood and her happiness. He glanced up from his newspaper. On the front page was a small photograph of Betsy when she was younger, with her dark curly hair down to her shoulders, looking very serious for the photographer. Violet wondered whether to mention the detective's visit and decided not to.

She heard a carriage coming up the driveway. It had to be Bea.

'I've got to leave now,' her husband said.

Bea came in, all country trees and moral goodness, and just for a second Violet felt stifled. This wholesomeness didn't acknowledge the totality of life. It was only a part of it. But then she saw Bea's smile and felt relieved. Such straightforward goodness. How could she question it? She looked out at the honeysuckle at the window, noticing that the leaves were covered in a dark mildew. They were becoming corrupted, she thought. She would have to do something about it. Some time. Not now.

'Have you heard about the women disappearing from the asylum?' Bea asked. 'Lucky you got out of there alive!'

'I met one of them in the asylum,' Violet said. 'Her photograph is in the newspaper today.'

'I saw it. What was she like?'

'Kind.' She hesitated. 'Another one I met, just before I was leaving, told me that Archie used to come to the asylum. Donna said that he would give the doctor money.'

Bea looked astonished. 'Honestly, Violet! And you believed her tittle tattle?'

Violet was surprised by the ferocity of Bea's reaction, how dismissive she was. But people were always surprising her. They were always acting out of character. People were complex and inconsistent – bad people doing good things, good people bad things.

'So you think it was just Donna spinning tales?'

'Of course. Archie is a good-looking man. These impoverished lunatics are bound to latch onto him in some way. She would have seen him visiting you and just made up this story about him visiting her. You don't really think for a moment Archie is mixed up in this?'

'Of course not!'

'Well, stop spouting this drivel. I do sometimes wonder if you really *are* mad as a cuckoo! Is that jam I see you've been making?'

Bea strode over to the oven and picked up a spoon and began stirring. Violet felt irrationally angry with her.

'Could you leave that, Bea? You shouldn't stir jam so much.'

'Of course.' Bea still had her back to her but Violet could sense a coldness in the hunch of her shoulders. Bea was not used to anyone speaking to her like that, especially meek, apparently loyal Violet.

Violet was mortified.

'Can I get you some tea?'

'Yes, please,' Bea said, plonking herself down in the chair, smiling widely, and all was right with the world again. A brief tiff, thought Violet, that was all. Nothing significant. But she felt sad as if something, even if it had not been broken, had developed a crack.

'And did Betsy, the murdered one, have anything else to say for herself?'

'Just that her husband had put her in there.'

'But that's interesting in itself.'

'What do you mean? We don't know anything about him.'

'Exactly. Invisible. It makes it all seem suspicious. It's bound to be him.'

'I suppose so.'

Bea shrugged her shoulders. Her silver hair was like the skin of a dappled pony, Violet thought, so smooth and shiny. She wanted to stroke it. Why was she thinking these strange, inconsequential thoughts, she wondered. The sun shone through the window, bringing out the dark undertones of Bea's grey hair. She looked at Bea with her capable manner, her unfeminine trousers, her unostentatious way of dressing that became her so. She loved the way she took over the kitchen, made it hers too. Bea was fundamentally good. Her only slight fault was a lack of insight into others. She was so resolutely herself, she took it for granted others were themselves, too.

'Everyone in the village is panicking. I don't see why. If he's going to get you, he probably will.'

'It's probably best to take precautions,' Violet said cautiously.

And for some reason this made them both laugh.

'Anyway, what does a murderer look like?' Bea said.

'Surely he would be easy to spot.'

'Horrible,' Bea said. ' I don't want to think about it!'

Bea was the epitome of the anti-psychopath, thought Violet – wouldn't dream of manipulating anyone. She would just give direct orders. If she wanted someone to do something for her she would treat them like a horse or dog.

'Well, you can't be the killer, Violet. You couldn't manipulate yourself out of a room.'

'That's a relief,' Violet replied. And they both laughed out loud, again.

CHAPTER 28

DETECTIVE BENEDICT PAID her another visit, this time when Archie was at home. Seeing the two men sit next to each other in the drawing room in the evening light, Violet was struck by how different they were. The detective was the opposite of Archie, she thought. Detective Benedict was precise and present. He had vivid, alert eyes that flashed with a kind of painful intelligence. It's as if he understands too much, she thought, and it hurts him to be so different from others. She saw Archie appraising him with cool eyes.

'We have discovered a body.'

'Betsy!' she exclaimed before she could stop herself.

'No, it's a Donna Wakefield. We believe she was killed a while before Betsy Moore disappeared. Donna's body has been found a mile away from here on the other side of the village by the church. Although we think she may have been moved from the place where she was actually killed. We found some traces of granite dust on her skin. I wondered if you would mind answering some questions?' He turned to Archie.

'Of course.'

'I believe you have visited the asylum, Lord Murray?'

'Only to visit my wife.'

Violet remained silent regarding what Donna had told her about his previous secret visits.

The detective turned to Violet. 'You were there for a while, is that correct, Lady Murray?'

'About a month.'

You were there at the same time as Betsy and Donna?'

Violet nodded.

'Did either of them talk to you?'

She wracked her brain. She felt so tired. 'Donna was a dancer,' was all she could say. But to her surprise he looked interested in this.

'Ah, I wonder if that's significant. The murderer cut off her feet.'

'Like "The Red Shoes".'

'I'm sorry?'

'Never mind. It's just a fairy story.'

She could see Detective Benedict trying not to look impatient with her.

'Betsy had a husband. Did she mention him?'

'Yes, I remember now. She said he had been very cruel to her.'

'Well, he has disappeared. We think he had a motive. A mistress. He didn't want Betsy home. Doubt we will see him again. Probably killed all three.'

'*Three?*'

'Well, apart from Donna, there is also Amy Louden, another released patient, who went missing earlier in the year. Like Betsy, we still haven't found her body. Sad cases. All attractive, vulnerable young women.' He stood up.

'I'll see you out,' Violet said. As his body stood in the doorway, blocking out the light, she felt oddly, misguidedly drawn to it, as if it would help her in some way.

'Make sure your door is locked at night, just in case.'

She nodded. One day, she thought, he may be able to protect me.

She felt bereft at his leaving when she returned to the kitchen to see Archie there. He was staring at her.

'Betsy or Donna didn't talk to you about anything else?' He was looking worried.

'You know what I'm like. Things become so uncertain.'

Archie came up and hugged her. 'You need to look after yourself. Be careful.'

'Yes,' she said. 'I know. I *am* careful.' She hesitated, then added, 'You know that delusion I had recently? The body of Betsy by the stream? That Clara told you about. I don't think it could have been. A delusion, I mean. There are too many coincidences.'

'Darling, it's all these missing women. They are causing you to imagine things. Remember how vivid those crawling insects on Felix's back seemed to you?'

'So you don't believe me?'

Her husband looked exasperated.

'Darling, this has all happened before. You are just seeing things.'

'That was months ago! Before I went to the asylum. You yourself said that the asylum had cured me. Look, let me show you where I saw it.'

'I'm tired. It's been a long day. Show me tomorrow.'

She wanted to scream at him, but that would make her seem more insane.

'Please, Archie,' she said. 'At least we can check whether it's there or not.'

'*It's not there, Violet. There is no body.*' He was shouting at her.

She felt increasingly detached as if she were looking at a married couple arguing from far above. It was odd, she thought, that she was the one who was supposed to be mad yet he was the one getting angry. However, his rage was understandable. He had stood by her when she was put away, sent her flowers. She looked out of the window. An owl flapped over the lawn, ghostly slow and laborious.

He seemed to concede. 'Look, I'll come with you in the morning. Before I go to work, all right?'

'Promise?'

'Promise.' He gave her his most winning smile. She so wanted to be reassured, given a reason to believe in his version of the truth.

That night she looked down at her skin. Her body looked pale and fleshy in the moonlight, so animal and disposable.

The next morning, Archie roused her from a deep sleep.

'Darling,' he said, 'show me where the body is.'

She took his hand.

She led him through the estate to the field at the back where Betsy had lain. There was just the stream. The body had disappeared. All other signs of the murder had vanished, too: the iron rings in the ground, the macabre swan's wing.

'She has gone,' she said.

'Yes,' he replied. He was then silent, waiting for her to say something. She knew what she had to say.

'I must have been mistaken, got confused.'

He put his arm around her. It felt heavy and cold and wrong in the bright morning air.

'Would you like me to call the doctor?'

She nodded, acquiescing. She couldn't risk Felix coming to harm again. These delusions were too real for her to fight them.

'I'll call the doctor when I get into work and make an appointment for today.'

CHAPTER 29

V IOLET WALKED INTO the village to the doctor's. It was a bright sunny day. She felt oddly disconnected. This is not happening to me again, she thought. I will not let this happen to me. If I can will it not to happen, it will not occur. She waited in the waiting room. She had left black traces of earth on the white carpet.

The doctor called her in with his deep Scottish voice but his face was still featureless. He had helped her the first time. Helped her become well by taking her to the asylum: it had been for the best. So she felt grateful: he knew about her and had seen her at her worst.

'What can I do for you, Lady Murray?'

He made no mention that her husband had called him, had told him all about what had happened. It was necessary to keep up the charade for both of them that she was in some way independent and making her own decisions. That she was not being ushered down an inexorable path once more.

'I'm seeing things again.'

'Can you tell me what kind of things?'

'I saw a body. Of a girl. On our estate.'

'On it?'

'Actually on the edge of it. Just outside, by a stream.'

'When was this?'

'A while ago.'

'Gosh. Poor thing!'

'I suppose so.' Her voice sounded dull.

'Did anyone else see this?'

'I took my husband there this morning.'

He was silent. Always waiting, she thought, probably always waiting for her to say what was inevitable.

'And it had gone.'

'I see.'

'But I know Betsy has gone missing from the asylum. Along with another woman earlier this year, an Amy Louden. And Donna's body has just been discovered on the other side of the village.'

He scribbled something down. He had a fountain pen, with dark blue ink. The pen was made of some kind of green malachite that glittered.

'What do you think it means?' she asked.

'Difficult to say. We don't want to jump to conclusions.'

She knew what he meant. Jump to conclusions that she was seeing things where nothing existed, creating stuff out of thin air, demonstrating that the intervening months of recovery had meant nothing. It was just the passing of time. Why should time change anything?

'No,' she said. 'We don't want to jump to conclusions.'

'It could be,' he continued, 'just a trick of the light. It's significant you saw the body at dusk. Water and shadows can play tricks. It could have been a reflection.'

'My reflection?'

'Indeed.'

She thought of the image. The eviscerated body, the sublime wonder of Betsy's open dark eyes. And the swan's wing. No it hadn't been a reflection. She tried to look as if she was convinced.

'Yes, perhaps it was. Yes. Perhaps it could have been.'

The doctor looked relieved.

'My feeling is it was just a trick of the light. And perhaps you were feeling tired.'

'Yes, I did feel weary.'

'Look, I can give you some laudanum. Take a spoonful, morning and evening. But be careful. No more. It is easy to take too much. The important thing is, if it happens again, let me know. And we can investigate it further. But it's very important that you relax and take plenty of bed rest.'

She stood up.

'Thank you, Doctor.' She took the brown bottle of laudanum. 'This has been very helpful.'

'Not at all, Lady Murray. And best wishes to Archie.'

Those were the words that rang in her head as she left the doctor's. 'Best wishes to Archie.' As if in some way this comment undermined the sanctity of her world, suggesting that she was actually in someone else's world.

As she walked back through the village, she wondered about returning to the field. She decided not to. She reached the house, where she saw Clara at the kitchen window, her hair glinting in the sun. She looked like a visitation, a hard angel, cut out from stained glass. Violet suddenly felt, I'm not ready to see her, not up to pretending to be normal. I'm too tired.

Without seeming to make a decision, she had turned and was walking back out towards the fields and forest. She walked through the wood, the trees gently brushing her cheeks. It had been a delusion, wasn't that what the doctor had said?

She found her breathing grow heavier. As she approached the stream it looked exactly the same as it had when she had shown Archie the scene earlier. The water flowed gently. She peered into the stream. There seemed to be no disturbance to the pebbles or indentation in the sandy bottom. She took off her shoes and socks and entered the water. It was freezing, like a wild animal biting into her flesh. She walked further into the water. The reflection of the sunlight on the water still concealed some of the bottom of the stream. If she could look directly down, using her body to shield the water from the sun, she could see the bottom clearly.

There were just some golden pebbles and a few jagged black rocks. Some delicate strands of green weeds, waving in the currents. Something had been caught on one of them, a thread of silver light. She bent down into the cold water, her hand feeling as if it had been turned to stone. She carefully plucked the weed, tugging it out of the pebbles. It came away quite easily.

Unable to bear the cold any longer, she staggered out of the water and collapsed onto the bank. Her legs had grown purple, but she was holding the weed tightly in her hand, slimy and cold, like a small slithering fish. She opened up her hand and there on her palm lay the weed, thin and delicate and frail. Caught up in the weed was a glittering piece of metal, a silver pendant in the shape of the letter B. She pulled the pendant out from the weed. B for Betsy. The pendant was cold and hard, and real to the touch of her skin.

Later, she hid the piece of jewellery in her jewellery box. They had taken all her secrets away from her in the asylum. They had shone a light on them and seized them for themselves.

CHAPTER 30

S HE RETURNED TO London and to Lavinia's grand house in Eaton Square, with the black ornate balconies and the walls white as icing on a wedding cake. To her surprise the butler let her in without question and again showed her up to the drawing room to wait. She picked up a book from a table. On the cover was a fine ink drawing: it clearly was a tattoo. A tattoo of a ship's wheel, the circle with the spokes of the wheel dissecting it. She touched the inky artifice of the wheel. The cover felt like skin, she thought. And now the wheel lay in the centre of a book's cover. She opened up the book. It was of a book of poems by Milton.

Lavinia came in to see her looking at it.

'A beautiful edition, don't you think?'

Violet nodded.

'Very rare.'

'Yes.'

'Where did you get it from?'

'I bound it for the wife of a captain whose body was washed up onto the shore. She never collected it from me. Some like to bind books in human skin as a keepsake. Can be of someone who is loved. A widow might bind her late husband's skin to remember him by, or a lost daughter.'

'How many of these collectors are there?'

She shrugged her shoulders.

'I have no idea . . .'

'It all sounds grotesque,' Violet said. 'Books bound in human skin.'

'Never underestimate the ingenuity of the human mind. What is it that Shakespeare says? "There are more things in heaven and earth, Horatio/Than are dreamt of in your philosophy." Physical transience comes second to the permanence of art and genius. Books take precedence over our insignificant human mortality.'

'How extraordinary.'

'Do you think so? It just seems sensible to me. Like keeping someone's hair in a locket. It's not so different. Archie asked if I would do this for him, too.'

'Do what?'

'Take some skin. To bind a book. I imagine it was the book you were asking about the last time you were here. He had a book of fairy tales he had been planning to give Rose on their first wedding anniversary. She had always loved fairy tales.'

'So you did? You bound a book in her skin?'

'Yes. It worked beautifully. I had to dry the skin first. And stretch it. She had pale skin. It took the green dye well. He wanted that piece of skin especially, to remind him of her. It took a while to do this. By the time I had finished, he had married you.'

Chapter 31

S HE HAD ALWAYS trusted him, his sense of convention. She had trusted him with her life. And she had believed in their marriage, she had believed that if they just both kept walking without looking down, they would get to the other side. She had let him into her heart when she should have erected barriers around it and built walls and dug a moat beneath and filled the moat with deep water.

One night she followed her husband down the road again. He walked through the forest but this time he didn't take the road to the asylum. He continued walking through the forest to a sheer rock face where a tunnel had been roughly hewn into its side. She watched as he disappeared into it. She found she couldn't go any further. She was scared of what she might discover. She ran back home and went to bed and slept long and dreamlessly.

The next night, she got out of bed. It was a moonlit night and she could see everything clearly. Archie was sound asleep. She got dressed and crept out of the house and went down the garden to the woods. At first she missed the tunnel and had to retrace her steps using a deformed tree, bent over low like a witch, as a marking post. At the entrance of the tunnel she could hear crying sounds or was it just the cry of an owl from far above? She entered the tunnel and came to a series of doors. She tried one, but it was locked.

'Is anyone here?' she cried out. But there was no answer. Then she heard music coming from inside one of the rooms. It was piano music, the sound of Schumann, one of his last sonatas. Was someone playing on the piano? Or was it a recording?

'Is anyone there?' she shouted over the music.

She walked back home, her heart pounding at what she was discovering about her husband. This new fairy story she had been plunged into against her will.

In the morning she came downstairs. She heard the same Schumann sonata she had heard in the cave coming from the piano in the drawing room. She went to the doorway. She recognised the golden hair of Clara's head as she bent over the piano. Had it been Clara who had been playing the piano in the cave? Violet quietly stepped away from the doorway.

Violet confronted Archie when he returned home.

'It's to do with the book,' she said. 'The book of fairy tales. You used Rose's skin. For the binding. And now you are murdering women taken from the asylum. And Clara is helping you. What are you doing with them?'

Archie looked at her astonished. 'Have you gone *completely* insane? What are you talking about? Using Rose's skin to bind a book does not make me a murderer! You need rest. Go to bed. I'll call a doctor.'

'I don't need a doctor.'

When she started screaming she found she couldn't stop.

Archie shouted out for Clara. A few moments later she came rushing in. Violet deliberately knocked over the velvet armchair to block Clara's way. It crashed to the floor. But it made no difference. What was substantial in the room were desires and fears. The air had become violent with possibility.

'Felix,' she shouted. 'What about Felix?'

They were both approaching her as she backed into the wall. How could she escape? She was struggling to think clearly.

'Felix will be fine,' Archie said.

They were about to grasp her when she heard the door open. Felix, small and intent, stood in the doorway.

'Mummy,' he said.

She nodded dumbly, trying not to cry, not to worry him. 'Go back to bed,' she whispered.

Clara quickly swept him up and she could hear them going upstairs.

Archie was now standing over her.

'What are you going to do, Archie?'

He smiled. 'Nothing. There's no need to worry. I am not going to harm you. You are in a delusionary state, dearest.'

His dark eyes looked fondly, almost flirtatiously, at her, trying to beguile and convince her, she thought.

'No,' she shouted. 'I'm fine. Leave me alone.'

She looked frantically around. She had to stop this. She saw a silver paperknife on a table and grabbed it. She flashed the blade at him and he took a step back.

'Don't be foolish, Violet. I'm going to do you no harm. I'm wanting to help you.'

Again that fresh innocent smile. She felt a moment's doubt. Was he right? Was this all fantasy? Had she gone mad again? But she kept the paperknife stretched out in front of her, aimed at Archie's chest to prevent him from coming any nearer.

She could see his confusion, his fear of her impulsiveness.

'I know all about you. Where you go to at night,' she cried.

'We both just want to help.'

'So you deny you know anything about these missing women?'

'Of course. Do I look like a murderer?'

She looked at him. No, he didn't look like a murderer. But hadn't that been the point all along, that Archie didn't look like a murderer. He had been different from how he appeared. He had always looked so plausible.

'If we take you to the asylum, they will be able to help you, to get you through this. It will be best for Felix. You want the best for him, don't you?'

How predictable of him, to use her weakest point, Felix.

'You don't want him to come to any harm again, do you?'

She felt the paperknife waver and Archie lurched forward and wrenched it from her hand. He then grabbed her roughly around the waist.

'No,' she screamed.

She struggled but he was far too strong for her. Clara returned downstairs and they pulled her up the stairs to bed still screaming. Archie forced open her mouth and Clara poured laudanum down her throat until she fell into a fitful sleep.

A few hours later she woke up. She looked at the clock: it was midnight. She heard noises downstairs. Someone had come into the house; that must have been what had woken her up. A few moments later there was a knock at the door and the local doctor came in, next to her husband. This time his face had features and she was astonished at how fair and young he looked. He smiled gently at her as if she were a patient. And she suddenly realised that she *was* a patient, that was what she had become again.

'Your husband called me, Lady Murray. He's worried about you.'

She simply looked at him, not knowing what to say, suddenly vulnerable lying in bed as the men in suits stood in the doorway.

'I mustn't look weak,' she thought. 'I mustn't start feeling paranoid. That is what they think I am. I must seem calm and sane.'

'It's nothing,' she said. 'It's a misunderstanding.'

The doctor came and sat down by the bed. She stared at his mouth. He took her hand and held it firmly, like a romantic lover, she thought. He measured her pulse.

'Her pulse is absolutely normal.'

'Yes,' she said. 'It would be.'

'Otherwise you're feeling fine?'

'Just a bit tired.'

'Your husband says you've been talking about a book, a book of fairy tales.'

But she saw the two men exchange glances. He had come *for* her, not to help.

'It's just a misunderstanding,' she repeated. 'He buys so many books.'

Yes, she thought, he buys so many books. She had got confused. Her heart was pounding. She had to appear normal.

'You've been ill for quite a while now, haven't you, since the birth of your son? But you are a lot better than you were. How long was your stay in the asylum?'

'Over a month,' Archie said.

'My husband. He is a book collector.'

The doctor produced a syringe from his bag. 'I know that, Violet.'

'You don't understand. The book of fairy tales. It's bound in Rose's skin.'

'You are hallucinating.'

'No. You must help me.'

But she could see the patient look in his eyes meant he didn't understand. The lack of natural incredulity meant he didn't believe the truth.

He injected her and, still struggling against the sleepiness, she whispered, '*Felix . . . Felix*,' before falling into unconsciousness.

CHAPTER 32

S HE WOKE UP in the asylum in the familiar long serge nightgown. She felt paradoxically relieved – perhaps it *was* all a delusion, these thoughts *were* insane. This was where she *belonged*.

The asylum doctor came in. He exuded his normal warmth and paternalism.

'This is the day of your new treatment.'

She was confused. 'What do you mean?'

'It's a pioneering method. It will stop any of those nasty delusions coming back.'

'How does it work?'

'Rewires your brain. Absolutely painless.' He smiled at her reassuringly.

Her heart was beginning to race. She remembered the woman in the wheelchair in the reception room. 'I don't want it.'

'I'm afraid you don't have any choice in the matter. I have discussed it with your husband and we both agree that this is what is best for you. You have to think of Felix, too. Your husband has signed the forms.'

She was feeling like she was going to be sick. 'He wouldn't want this for me.'

'He just wants to help you. As we all do. Help care for your baby.'

'Let me see the forms.'

He showed them to her. There was Archie's signature, clearly written, giving his consent. She started to scream. The doctor immediately grabbed her, called for the nurse and they held her down on the bed while he gave her another injection. She felt the cold liquid course through her veins.

'Just a sedative. To help you sleep.' And after a while she became infused by a feeling of calm, and her hands fell still.

CHAPTER 33

WHEN SHE WOKE up she was in a high hospital bed, in part of the asylum she had never seen before, in a brightly lit room. Her legs and wrists were tied by shackles to the bedposts. A leather helmet encased her head. Wires led from her forehead to a machine on a trolley by the side of the bed.

The nurse came in. Her eyes seemed too big for her head, Violet thought, like large orbs. They were dark brown, like the fake eyes on an owl's wings, and they stared unblinkingly at her. Violet looked down at her own body covered by a coarse cream linen shift of rough cotton, that oddly gave her some comfort, as its roughness on her skin reminded her of her own flesh. The nurse was wearing a blue uniform, with a crisp apron as white as snow and a little cap perched on her head. Violet, because of those eyes, could imagine her head rotating right round, like the other nurse's had.

'Are you feeling better?'

Violet nodded. It was coming back to her, the fear of her husband. She heard the voice in her head saying, '*He will want to kill you, too.*' Standing by her bed the doctor was examining the machine and carefully adjusting the dials.

'We'll start off at a low voltage, nurse.'

She tried to move her lips, to say that she was sane, but

found there was a leather strap binding her mouth. The doctor looked down over her.

'Don't worry, Lady Murray, you will be perfectly fine. The leather is to stop you biting down on your tongue. We don't want you hurting yourself. This is only going to take a few minutes.'

Her eyes widened with fear. The light in the room was so bright. She couldn't move. They were bustling about and talking in low whispers. She could do nothing to help herself. She was powerless. Her eyes filled with tears of absolute fear. How did they know that the treatment would not harm her? It might eradicate who she was. It seemed so unpredictable.

The doctor turned the dial and a flash of light went through her head, like lightning. It was as if the entire world had exploded in a globe of light. *This is what death is* and then blackness.

She regained consciousness with the room slowly coming into focus again. The nurse at the machine still had her back to her, as if no time had passed. The doctor was looking down at Violet, his forehead furrowed. Her whole body was aching and she had the worst headache she had ever known. *But I don't feel any different,* she thought triumphantly. As if reading her mind, the doctor quickly took out his notebook and made some notes registering her reaction. This was where insanity lay, she thought, in his taking down of notes.

He turned to the machine. Tears again started to pour down her face. Her head began shaking, *no, no, stop it,* but she had been silenced and the doctor turned the dial higher. She felt like a horrible nightmarish mechanical toy, at the whim of her human master. Except he wasn't human, he was less human than she was.

Her whole body shook. Her body arched as much as the restraints would allow and she felt the hard leather strap between her lips and teeth as she bit down. She lost control of her bladder and the sheets grew warm and wet around her. The neural rebirth of her brain took on the form of fire. Pyrotechnic blooms of thought. A flashing light illuminated her brain, as if she had become the sun. It was a kind of ecstasy and she thought, life will never be the same again.

CHAPTER 34

WHEN SHE WOKE up, Archie was standing by her bed. He was giving her his grin that always disarmed her but at the same time she thought, why is he smiling? What is there to be smiling about?

'Hello darling,' he said.

'Hello.'

She tentatively sat up in bed. Her head ached fiercely. What was she doing in hospital? She couldn't remember coming here. There was also some indefinable difference about her. What was it? A lightness of heart, a feeling of peace. It felt blissful, as if a critical witch in her head had flown away up into the sky.

'Where's Felix?'

'He's at home. With Clara.'

She felt surprised. She had never heard of Clara before but he said the name as if she should know who Clara was. He saw the puzzlement on her face.

'Clara is someone I've brought in, to help you look after Felix.'

'But I keep telling you, I can manage on my own. I *like* to manage on my own. Care for him myself.'

'Clara is very well trained. She's an experienced nanny. She came with excellent credentials.'

'Who from?'

'Oh, it was the Richmonds, I think. Or was it the Bennets? I can't quite remember. But they were excellent.'

She felt too relaxed to argue. In fact it would be nice to have someone to help her look after Felix. Clara could be a companion for her, too. Archie was away so much.

'Thank you,' she said. 'I must admit, it will be a help.'

'Not at all. You and Clara will get on like a house on fire. Come on, let's take you away from this place! I've brought you your clothes.'

Archie left her alone in the room and a few minutes later she heard, through the door, Archie talking to the doctor. There were intense murmurings. She got out of bed and dressed. Archie and the doctor came back into the room. They both quickly smiled encouragingly at her. She was surprised to see that they seemed quite close friends. The doctor examined her head with his cold hands.

'There are just a couple of burn marks here, on the frontal lobes. They will fade soon. I expect a full recovery in a few weeks. Until then, I advise bed rest at home.' He addressed these comments to Archie, not to her.

'Don't worry, Doctor, I'll take good care of her,' Archie replied, shaking the doctor's hand, as if they had just made a successful business deal.

'Thank you so much, Doctor.'

'Feeling better, eh, Lady Murray? You look so much happier.'

'Absolutely,' she said.

'Is there any medication she needs to take with her?' Archie asked.

'Just the laudanum,' he said. 'And some ointment for the burns. And she will need help at home with the baby, I should imagine.'

'Oh, don't worry, I have already arranged that. A most suitable woman.'

'Excellent.' She could see the doctor thinking what a wonderful husband she had, how fortunate she was. Seeing him show his ostentatious love for her in front of the doctor, she thought, yes, indeed, how fortunate I am.

At first it was strange to be back home. Everything now looked brighter, more colourful, as if the world, instead of her, had been electrified. A gap seemed to have opened up between her and her perceptions, as if her feelings had in some way been displaced. She felt in a protective cocoon that shielded her from the coarseness of reality. When she held Felix, she was surprised by how much older he had grown. She felt a warm affection towards him, but the anxiety intertwined with the love had disappeared. As if she had been given back herself and the inner turmoil had gone. She knew she used to be more intelligent than she was now but some of the most intelligent people she had known were also the most miserable.

She applied her makeup carefully that evening, in the bedroom, before dining with Archie. Men had always found her attractive and they had never understood why. She didn't really understand why. She was growing older, but she still had the shape of desire, just in a more shadowy and obscure form. She opened up her jewellery box to look for some earrings. She found a silver pendant that she didn't recognise as hers. It was a B for Betsy, she remembered, and the image of a swan's wing came into her head.

She began to imagine what it would be like with Archie in bed that night, his body, his touch, what he would do to her, what she could do to him. How they could give each other pleasure. She loved to give and take pleasure. And she had not done that with Archie in so very long.

~

Archie collected the book of fairy tales back from Lavinia for the fourth time.

'It looks wonderful,' he said.

'I'm proud of it, too,' Lavinia said. 'I've spent care stretching and sewing. Look how smooth it is.'

She drew a finger over the cover and caressed the insert of the almost-but-not-quite-full moon.

'Fairy tales,' she said. 'Rose would have loved it. Rose loved fairy tales.'

A week after coming back from the asylum, Violet was in the drawing room, embroidering. She turned round to see Archie in the doorway. Her heart leapt: he was the husband she loved, the man she had chosen to spend her life with.

'I have a present for you,' he said.

He came over to her and gave her a book.

'You need to be careful. You don't want to be holding it like that. It's only recently been bound. It's a book of fairy tales.'

He traced over the cover with his hand and then bent down and kissed it. How strange he was with these books. The cover was of green vellum. A circle had been cut out of the calfskin on the front cover, the hole partially filled in with crescent-shaped segments in different shades of white and off-white, inserted one after another like a waxing moon. One of these slivers bore the remnant of a snakeskin scar.

'The moon isn't quite full,' she said.

'It will be soon,' he said and gave her a light smile.

She opened the fairy tale book up at the flyleaf and read the dedication.

'Who is Rose?' she asked.

'My first wife. She died in childbirth. She said she liked fairy tales because they reminded her of real life.' He laughed. 'So typical of Rose.'

'But I, too, think they are life-like,' Violet said. There is a psychic truth about them.' A shadow crossed her light-filled mind, a sudden memory of how she had been, which dissipated as quickly as it had come.

Archie laughed. 'You mustn't think like that. It doesn't suit you.'

She thought he might have liked her being similar to Rose, but clearly not. She looked into his dark blue eyes. He was everything to her. Her past, present and future. Why would she want anything but this fairy tale she was in? Rose had been unlucky, tragically unlucky. There was no reason why she, Violet, would be so. No reason why luck, this time, wouldn't be on her side. She had never done anyone any harm, had never betrayed anyone. Did she not deserve happiness, a gift for being a good person? Perhaps in some way Rose had not been good, had received the fate she had deserved. Violet's fate would be different.

She put the book down. That night, Archie held her tightly in his arms and she could sense his animal smell and dived into it, like a fish leaping in a pond, flicking its tail and then sinking deep until all she saw was resolute and comforting blackness, lips pressed against lips and hands delving, his body sinuous and shining.

Her son became like a shadow beneath the grandiose statue of their love and passion. She struggled to love and care for her son, to come out of the shadows of her marriage, but the love for her son couldn't compete with the blinding light of the new intimacy she now shared with her husband.

Chapter 35

G OING TO BED that evening, she walked past one of the bathrooms. The door had been left ajar and Violet could see Clara's reflection clearly in the bathroom mirror. Her blonde hair was tied up loosely in a bun to keep it out of the water. Tendrils hung down over her shoulders. In the mirror Violet could see how large her breasts were, naked and uncontained. Clara looked undone: voluptuous, overflowing with an abundance of flesh and sensuality, this plethora of sensuality.

Violet turned away. She continued down the passageway to the marital bedroom. She quietly slipped into bed and lay there alone, between the dry cotton sheets, waiting for Archie to come up, but thinking of the density of Clara's figure, its material presence, its physicality. She looked down between the sheets at her own thin, unforgiving, narrow form and wondered how she and Clara could be the same species. She caressed her hip bones, her elbows, her soft belly left rounded after Felix.

She was now a woman of two halves, half woman, half mother. Two bodies from different times conjoined. But Clara was still whole, of a single time, her body still existing for a single purpose, to give and take pleasure. Her body had not been divided in half by motherhood. It was Clara who had singularity of purpose.

~

She and Clara met in the hallway in the morning.

'You look ill,' Clara said suddenly.

'No – I'm fine.'

Why did Clara's concern seem slightly over-bearing? Where was that shrill anarchic voice inside her head coming from, she wondered? And then a quick feeling of calm swept over her.

'Do you want to take a rest?'

'No, honestly, I'm fine.' She was shouting now.

Clara looked taken aback. She had to control herself. Her hands were sweating. She could feel the skin congealing in her clutched palms, as if it were melting. As if she were melting. She suddenly hated Clara. Her self-contained manner. She wanted to wipe that placid smirk from her face. Make her feel for one second how Violet felt all the time. She felt sick and suddenly the room tunnelled into blackness. The floor came up to meet her. Everything became black.

'Are you all right?' It was the soft voice of Clara.

Violet came round, sitting in a chair, in the kitchen. Clara was bending over her. Clara's pretty tendrils seemed intertwined with flowers, her young fresh face, seemingly unaffected by the heat, pale and luminous at the same time.

Clara took a glass from the table and quickly washed it under the tap. It was only a glass, Violet thought. Why did she imagine it shattering in Clara's small capable hands, and cutting her? The blood draining down, mingling into the water. Why was she associating English rose Clara with blood? Her thoughts weren't making any sense.

'Where is Felix?' The words sounded so anxious, border-line hypnotised.

'He's with his little friend James, remember, in the village? He's staying a few days there.'

'Of course. I'd forgotten.'

She still felt angry with Clara, at her unflappable pragmatism. It felt callous.

Violet could see the young woman's full breasts beneath her dress. She wondered what would happen if she deliberately undid the small pearly buttons down the front of Clara's dress. Would she be able to see the shape of her pale nipples beneath? Would she be able to slip the breasts out, smooth and round?

She caught Clara looking at her. She had an odd complicit smile on her face.

Oh, my Lord, had she read her mind?

She watched as Clara handed her a glass of water. Her head was beginning to throb.

She wondered when reality would come and seize her or was it already doing so? Insidious whispering in her ear, shadowing her while all the time she was deliberately ignoring what reality was saying to her, having nothing to do with it. She, like Rose, wanted a fairy tale. The fairy tale that was her family, her love for her husband, his love for her and their beloved precious son that made their family whole. She had forgotten all about the hallucinations, the over-riding desire to harm her son, the flashes of light. Yes, she had forgotten all about it. It was Clara who was the wicked stepmother.

CHAPTER 36

THE FOLLOWING MORNING Violet came into the kitchen and saw Clara, her back to her, standing at the pantry bringing out some milk. Archie was lounging on a kitchen chair, his legs wide apart, staring at the curve of Clara's waist. It was as if a snake had wrapped itself around the man she had once known, or swallowed him whole so she could just see the outline now, clothed in snakeskin.

Violet wondered about love, how people who weren't loving were incapable of understanding the wonder of others. About selfishness that didn't understand unselfishness, in fact despised it as weakness. And 'the corrupt'. Did they despise innocence? Or long for it. Want to corrupt it. Make the blameless the same as they were. Did innocence disturb them, make them feel wrong, hold up a mirror to their own distorted faces? And how guiltless was she? How much of her innocence was a shield from her fear of the truth?

Clara turned round to smile at Violet. She had taken Clara's integrity for granted, had stared at her milkmaid face and assumed everything. She looked through the kitchen window at the estate. Assumption. She had assumed her whole life, the geography of the place, the permanence of her family. She had never envisaged a different future, rather presumed it, the presumption of innocence.

~

Fairy tales, it was all to do with fairy tales. She went back to the fairy tale book he had given her and opened it and read. Her eyes alighted on the story called 'The Constant Tin Soldier'. She thought of Archie and his mechanical, almost military ways. He was the soldier and Clara the ballerina doll. She started to read some of the other stories, 'The Wild Swans', 'The Little Mermaid' and 'The Red Shoes'.

Her heart pounding, she went into the drawing room where Archie was in his armchair, reading. She could now picture the chair having fallen over.

'I've remembered everything.'

He met her gaze. 'We are a happy family now.'

'It is all illusion. The house. The money. The security. It is based on quicksand. On your lies and smoke and mirrors. Thinking I was loved and protected. I am part of your illusion,' she said, as if someone else, someone who was truly protecting her, was speaking through her lips.

'I don't know what you are talking about.' He gave her a clumsy smile and for a moment she believed him. *How she wanted to believe him*. She thought, yes, I am mad. How can this engaging man, such a loving father to Felix, be so monstrous? Archie, the father to her child. Where were these malicious thoughts coming from? How could she be so disloyal? He was her life, their lives interwoven like a pattern in a tapestry. If one thread were pulled out, their whole life would unravel. He was so precious to her. She could not imagine her life without him. This was what marriage meant, the indissolubility of their lives. She was lost without him and she had long thought that he would be nothing without her.

It is not he who is mad. It is me. She felt faint with uncertainty. Archie was quick to notice her self-doubt.

'Violet, you are tired. You've only just come back from your treatment in the asylum.'

'Clearly it hasn't worked,' she said quietly.

'Give me the book back,' he said.

She stood staring at him. 'It is only a book of fairy tales. I'll put it back in the library.'

Why, she wondered, had he married her? Was it to do with giving him a son and heir? He would never get over the love he felt for his first wife. She would always be in Rose's shadow.

'Rose is like the Ice Queen. She has left a shard of ice in your heart. Clara is just your plaything and accomplice.'

'I will never forget Rose lying there, our dead baby cradled in her arms. I knew soon they would both be buried deep under the earth, that I would never hold or caress her again. Her skin looked translucent, like marble. I bent down to feel it. It was as white as marble, too. I stroked it. I thought, I will never stroke this skin again. It looked so beautiful.

'After a photograph was taken of them, I was left alone with them both to grieve. I pulled up her gown. I took the knife they had used to sever the dead baby's umbilical cord and cut a piece of skin around her swollen uterus, and pulled it back. It came away easily. There was only a little blood. I knew then what I wanted to do. I wanted to create a token of my love for her.'

'What about the other women? The women from the asylum?'

'Don't you see? She loved fairy tales so much. The moon was decoration. Besides, they were all mad, those women. They had nothing to live for. You will join them. To make the moon full.'

'And what fairy tale would I be in?'

'Haven't you realised? Isn't it obvious?' He traced her face with his finger. 'Your face has such beautiful skin.'

'I'm not the sick one,' Violet said. 'You should be the one in the asylum. I will not be put in a fairy tale.'

'It is not up to you.'

She thought quickly: she had no choice but to seem to acquiesce.

'If I agree to this, will you and Clara look after Felix for me?'

He smiled. 'Of course. We should all have dinner together tonight,' he continued. 'You, me and Clara. To celebrate everything.'

He came over and held her tight. 'I knew in the end you would understand,' he whispered, 'how important this book is to me. How vital it is to complete its decoration.'

Chapter 37

A SENSE OF an ending came upon her. It had to be as well thought out as the moon on the cover of the fairy tale book. She felt impelled to bring the ending about. What had happened was unbearable, the realisation of her husband's monstrosity, his and Clara's illicit relationship.

She still felt in a state of shock and the world seemed distant. Her feelings of jealousy for Clara had long ago receded. Clara hardly impinged on her and was not even worthy of her contempt. Clara had taken part in her husband's evil deeds, slept with him and, with a clarity of cold insight, Violet realised that Clara and Archie deserved each other. Those who betray others, lie and deceive, deserve each other. Like an algebraic equation they are equal to each other and cancel each other out. It was only she and Felix who were left, who remained in the story.

And this realisation made her ending clearer, what it was exactly she was compelled to do. So Archie wanted to put her in a fairy tale. Well, she would put him in one instead. She remembered the ending of 'The Tin Constant Soldier', the story where Archie and Clara belonged. But how to rewrite this fairy tale? Her husband's and his lover's physical strength were so much greater than her own. She needed a secret potion, a sleeping draught.

She put the book back on the shelf and ran upstairs to their bedroom. She snatched the small brown medicine bottle from her bedside table – it was still at least two-thirds full. She knew she would have to act quickly. Archie was on a trajectory to complete the pattern on the book. Tonight might be her final chance.

She looked again at the bottle in her hand and her heart went cold. She could not go through with this. She should contact the detective. He would help. But would he believe her? She had been put in an asylum – twice. It was her word against her husband's and the doctors' and even the capable Clara's. No one had believed her before. They would not believe her now. No, the detective would not help her, there would be no prince coming to her rescue. She had to finish this story herself.

She was no longer sure if what she was about to do was for revenge or self-preservation or both and she hardly cared. She only knew that this story had to be completed. She was acting in a purely intuitive way as if her imaginative reading of 'The Constant Tin Soldier' was the only source of truth and reality. Lucid thought or logic would only serve to obfuscate her, confuse the moral rightness of what she had to do. For fairy tales had their own morality, their own cruel sense of right and wrong that pierced any mundane surface.

That evening, Violet dressed for dinner wearing her favourite red satin gown and tied her hair up. It would be the first time Clara would formally dine with them. Violet took the small bottle of laudanum from her bedroom table and hid it beneath the sash at her waist. She went down to the kitchen where the cook was preparing dinner and, while her back was turned, took out the bottle from underneath her sash. She carefully poured all the liquid contents into the tureen of spinach soup.

As husband and wife waited at the table for Clara to come

down, Violet could see her husband looking at her admiringly in the candlelight. When Clara entered the dining room, to Violet's surprise her youthful surface looked slightly dulled. Violet had imagined she would look triumphant. It was as if that now her affair with Violet's husband was no longer secret, Clara had lost some of her magical power and vigour.

She wore a blue velvet dress and her hair was pulled tightly back so that her features looked heavy and insolent rather than seductive. Violet wondered if Clara cared that she would never be able to replace Rose in Archie's heart.

The cook poured out the soup. While Violet pretended to sip hers, she watched as her husband and his lover finished every last drop from their bowls.

'How was the soup?' she asked Archie.

'Delicious,' he replied but she could see his eyelids beginning to droop.

'You look tired, my darling,' she said.

She turned to Clara whose head was nodding forward.

'I think you both need to rest.'

The cook came in to clear the bowls. Violet realised she had to get the servants to leave the house. They were innocent. She saw the cook notice how dazed Archie and Clara were beginning to look.

'I think we are all tired. We have had enough to eat. Is there not a dance tonight in the village?' Violet asked.

The cook smiled, a large woman who was still relatively young and had great enthusiasm for small pleasures. Her plump face creased up in a wide smile.

'There is, Lady Murray. In the hall.' The cook glanced up at the mantelpiece clock. It said nine o'clock.

'It's just beginning,' the cook said, hopefully.

'Why don't you take yourself and the housemaids off for the evening? Have some fun!'

The cook looked doubtfully at the uncleared table. 'What about the table, Your Ladyship?'

'Leave it until tomorrow. The dishes will still be there in the morning.'

Violet looked down at the ancestral plates, the empty soup bowls with the Murrays' crest. She remembered the one she had broken. Was that how this had all started, like the pricking of a finger on a spinning wheel? How long ago it all now seemed.

'Lord Murray and Clara do seem tired,' the cook added, rather anxiously.

'Don't worry. I will take them up to their rooms. It's been a long day for all of us. I am going to retire early, too. I'll leave the front door unlocked for you. I don't expect you to be back before midnight.'

'Many thanks, Lady Murray.'

'Goodbye.'

The cook looked startled. Violet realised she had sounded too final. 'Have a lovely time,' Violet added cheerfully.

'Good night, Lady Murray.'

Violet remained sitting in the dining room until she heard all the servants leave, laughing and slamming the door behind them. Archie and Clara were still propped up in their chairs, now barely conscious, like apparitions of death, she thought. They were both in their finery as the candles were burning down and the silver knives were twinkling in the flickering light. Their faces had grown pale like ghosts and their eyes glassy, just like a tin soldier and toy ballerina, she thought.

'I need to take you up to the bedroom now,' she said.

Clara murmured, 'I love you, Archie,' in a way, Violet thought, that she had never murmured to him. With such an intense knowledge of him, born of passion. Violet, in contrast, had mostly loved him like a dependent child.

Violet stood and went over to Clara and gently pulled her up from her chair. The blue velvet of Clara's dress brushed gently against her bare arms. Clara's arms looked so white compared to hers. Violet led her – how meek she was – upstairs to their marital bedroom, undressed her and unlaced her corset, releasing her breasts.

Violet pulled back the heavy brocade coverlet of their bed and laid the sleeping naked Clara down in it. The bed where Rose had given birth to her stillborn child, where Violet had given birth to Felix. Had Clara, too, been in this bed before, she wondered? Perhaps when Violet had been locked up in the asylum.

Violet returned to the dining room. Archie had now slumped forward on the table, his chestnut curls dangerously near a still-burning candle. She moved the candlestick away.

'Be careful, darling. You don't want to catch fire,' Violet said softly.

Mustering all her strength, she pulled him to his feet, enjoying the warm heaviness of his masculine body leaning against her.

'Clara is waiting for you in our bed,' she said.

As she and Archie climbed the stairs together and he leaned on her for support he muttered, 'You have been such a good mother to Felix, Violet. I know you have always done your best.'

'But have I been a good wife?' she asked.

'You are a wonderful wife, Rose. You are the love of my life.'

'By any other name,' Violet replied softly.

She took him into the bedroom, undressed him too, and laid him next to Clara.

'This is where you both belong, now,' she said softly.

She intertwined their arms. How in love they looked, she

thought. She gently pulled the coverlet over their unconscious bodies. In the flickering gas-light they both looked dead, she thought, when really they were just in a deep sleep. She shut the door behind her and locked it with the key.

She went downstairs to the library. She pulled out some of the books from the shelves and built a pile of them in the middle of the floor until it reached her waist. She perched the fairy tale book on the top. She took a match and lit its cover and watched as the circular moon of the pale skin inserts turned black and shrivelled, as the gilt-edged pages of the book then also caught fire. Soon the green dye began to run, revealing the pale skin of the binding. The colours of the illustrations melted into one another. The white flare of paper burning grew larger, the pages of other books in the pile rustling as they caught fire, one by one. Soon all the books in the pile were burning, the heat in the library growing intense and the room becoming an inferno of light and fury.

The heat at last drove her out. She fled the house, into the cold moonlight. Only when she reached the end of the driveway did she finally look back. The entire lower floor of their house was on fire, the flames licking up towards the second floor and the roof and into the night sky.

Violet turned away and started to walk down the road to the village. She needed to collect Felix from his friend's. She looked down at her blackened hands covered in soot and burns. She would not mention the book of fairy tales to anyone, for she knew that if she did, they might return her to the asylum. She looked up at the full white moon in the sky and wondered what it saw.

ACKNOWLEDGEMENTS

Thanks to Chris and Jen Hamilton-Emery, and to Jenny Brown, and to Regi Claire and Ron Butlin. And to my mother.

ALSO AVAILABLE FROM SALT

ALICE THOMPSON
Justine (978-1-78463-031-7)
The Falconer (978-1-78463-009-6)
The Existential Detective (978-1-78463-011-9)
Burnt Island (978-1-907773-48-8)

NEW FICTION FROM SALT

MORE FICTION FROM SALT

ELIZABETH BAINES
Too Many Magpies (978-1-84471-721-7)
The Birth Machine (978-1-907773-02-0)

RON BUTLIN
Ghost Moon (978-1-907773-77-8)

LESLEY GLAISTER
Little Egypt (978-1-907773-72-3)

ALISON MOORE
The Lighthouse (978-1-907773-17-4)
The Pre-War House and Other Stories (978-1-907773-50-1)
He Wants (978-1-907773-81-5)

CHRISTOPHER PRENDERGAST
Septembers (978-1-907773-78-5)

SHORT STORIES FROM SALT

ELIZABETH BAINES
Used to Be (978-1-78463-036-2)

CARYS DAVIES
The Redemption of Galen Pike (978-1-907773-71-6)

STELLA DUFFY
Everything is Moving, Everything is Joined:
The Selected Stories of Stella Duffy (978-1-907773-05-1)

CATHERINE EISNER
A Bad Case and Other Adventures of Disturbed Minds
(978-1-84471-962-4)

MATTHEW LICHT
Justine, Joe and the Zen Garbageman (978-1-84471-829-0)

KIRSTY LOGAN
The Rental Heart and Other Fairytales (978-1-907773-75-4)

DAN POWELL
Looking Out Of Broken Windows (978-1-907773-73-0)